D1014552

MARVEL CINEMATIC UNIVERSE
PHASE TWO

MARVEL CINEMATIC UNIVERSE
PHASE TWO

MARVEL

GUARDIANS OF THE GALAXY

Adapted by **CHRIS WYATT** and **ALEX IRVINE**

Based on the Screenplay by **JAMES GUNN**

Story by **NICOLE PERLMAN** and **JAMES GUNN**

Produced by **KEVIN FEIGE**, p.g.a.

Directed by **JAMES GUNN**

LITTLE, BROWN AND COMPANY
New York   Boston

Little, Brown and Company
Hachette Book Group
1290 Avenue of the Americas, New York, NY 10104
Visit us at lb-kids.com

Little, Brown and Company is a division of Hachette Book Group, Inc.
The Little, Brown name and logo are trademarks of Hachette Book Group, Inc.

The publisher is not responsible for websites (or their content) that are not owned by the publisher.

First Edition: November 2015

ISBN: 978-0-316-25675-9

10 9 8 7 6 5 4 3 2 1

RRD-C

Printed in the United States of America

PROLOGUE

It was very cold on Peter Quill's last day on planet Earth. It was so cold that the nine-year-old could almost see his breath indoors.

Sitting on a hard plastic bench listening to his Awesome Mix Tape Vol. 1 on headphones he'd gotten for Christmas, Peter looked down and fiddled with the buttons on his tape player. He tried not to think about where he was, in a hospital where his mother lay sick. Very sick. She'd been seeing doctors for a long time, and Peter had almost gotten used to the way she sometimes called him by the wrong name, or forgot things he knew she knew.

But now the family was gathered in the room, Gramps and Peter's aunts, and Peter knew things were much worse. He tried to sink away into the music and not think about it.

"Peter, your mama wants to speak with you."

Peter looked up to see Gramps kneeling in front of him. How long had he been there? Peter didn't move. He knew what would happen if he stopped listening to the music. It was the only thing that stood between him and...

"Come on, Pete. Let's take these fool things off," Gramps said, removing Peter's headphones. His voice was firm but warm. He stopped the tape and put the player and headphones in Peter's backpack as he walked Peter into his mother's room. He couldn't see his mother from the door. All he could see was the bed and the beeping machines and the worried women clustered around the bed.

Gramps stood back as Peter walked around the bed and stood where his mother could see him. He could hear her breathing, slow and wheezy. She tried to lift up her head and greet him. Her hair was gone from one of the treatments the doctors had given her, and her skin was pale.

Peter could see the shapes of her bones under the skin. She had some trouble focusing her eyes, but when she looked at him she smiled a little. He saw her looking at his face, and her smile slipped a little when she noticed the bruise under his eye.

She frowned at the welt and asked, "Why have you been fighting with the other boys again, baby?" Her voice was barely above a whisper.

Peter shrugged.

"Peter?" she prompted. He didn't want to say anything to worry her, but Peter had never been able to keep anything from his mother. They were a team, especially since his father wasn't around.

"They hurt a little frog that ain't done nothing," Peter said, trying to explain about the bullies in his neighborhood. He looked down and away from her, embarrassed and scared and unsure of what to do. "They smushed it with a stick."

"You're so like your daddy," Mama whispered. "You even look like him." Her eyes drifted up toward the skies, a dreamy expression crossing her face. "And he was an angel composed out of pure light."

Peter didn't know what she meant. He didn't know

what his daddy looked like because he'd never seen him—
but deep inside he was glad to hear it. Out of the corner
of his eye he saw Gramps exchange a quick look with one
of Peter's aunts, a look that said, *She's getting "confused"
again.*

"Meredith," Gramps said, trying to bring her back.
"You've got a present there for Peter, don't you?"

She looked dazed for a moment as her vision of angels
faded away, but then Mama looked down at the present
sitting on the bedsheets.

Mama stared down into her lap as if seeing the present
for the first time. "Of course," she said. She tried to pick up
the package, but she didn't have the strength.

Peter took it in his hands and looked at the sloppy pack-
aging and crooked bow. "I got you covered, Pete," Gramps
said as he picked up the present and stuck it in Peter's open
backpack.

"You open it up when I'm gone, okay?" she whispered.
Peter was trying to be brave, but when she said that he felt
his eyes start to get hot and sting with tears. He didn't want
to cry in front of her. Not now.

"Your grandpa is gonna take such good care of you, at
least until your daddy comes back to get you."

She swallowed deeply and then held out her hand to Peter. "Take my hand, baby."

Peter looked at Mama's hand, turned palm up on the blanket. He wanted to take it, he wanted to touch her one last time, but he knew if he touched her it would make everything real. If he could hold back, maybe that would stop it all from happening. He turned his face away, tears rolling down his cheeks.

"Pete, come on," Gramps said.

"Take my hand, baby," Mama said once again. Peter was trying to work himself up to do it when she hitched her breath and then let out a long sigh. The beeping sound from the machine next to her bed turned into a steady drone and Mama's eyes drifted shut.

"No," he said. "No." He kept saying it over and over again, building up until he was screaming. No, he should have taken her hand. No, she couldn't be gone. She couldn't be dead. She couldn't have left him all alone. No.

Gramps picked him up and Peter thrashed, still screaming as Gramps carried him back out into the hallway. A doctor rushed into the room past them. Gramps set him down, and Peter saw that Gramps was crying, too. "Pete," he said. "Just stay here. Okay? Please?"

Gramps turned and walked slowly back into Mama's room—no, not Mama's room. The room where Mama had been before she died.

No, Peter thought. It couldn't be real. None of it could be real.

That's when Peter ran.

He didn't think about running. He just did. No one stopped him.

He burst through the hospital's outside door and ran across the parking lot. When he got to the field on the other side of the parking lot, he kept running. A cold fog swirled around him, and his shoes were soon soaked from the wet grass, but he continued. When he finally was out of breath, he dropped to his knees and sobbed. No one came looking for him. He was alone.

A deep groan came from above him and the wind kicked up, blowing the fog away. A brilliant light shone down on him, too bright to look at directly. He squinted through the wind and his tears, seeing the outline of something incredible.

It was a giant spaceship, the size of a jet plane or even bigger, hovering in the air over him. Its wings spread out to cover most of the field, and it was tipped down so its nose pointed directly at Peter. Astonished, he froze there, unable to believe what he was seeing. Lights pulsed on the outside of the craft.

The beam of light tightened its focus on Peter and began to swirl in a storm of color. He cried out, but the light picked him up and stole him away.

CHAPTER 1

The planet Morag was once home to a great civilization. For centuries, the citizens worked together to develop commerce, build monuments, and advance the arts. But at the height of its culture, Morag's environment went through a terrible shift.

Violent storms of unimaginable power blasted the globe. Mega-earthquakes struck, sea levels rose and continents flooded, and the planet's crust shifted and became so unstable that nothing could live there anymore. The inhabitants evacuated the planet, scattering across the galaxy to whatever new homes they could find. They left behind everything they had built. Over the centuries, cities fell into ruins, flooded and destroyed by surging oceans and catastrophic earthquakes. The only visitors were adventurers or archaeologists who could brave Morag's turbulent oceans...and the occasional unfortunate survivor of a spacefaring accident.

But over time, the planet's upheaval lessened. Its seas receded again, exposing long-submerged ruins. Those ruins brought a different kind of visitor. Anyone who came to Morag still had to be brave and tough, but the ability to breathe water was no longer required. Now the planet's abandoned riches were there for the taking.

A ship curved down through Morag's stormy atmosphere and braked into a landing at the edge of a canyon. It locked itself down with heavy pins shot into the rock, holding the ship steady against the howling winds. Its ramp lowered and the pilot emerged into the storm, walking down the remains of an ancient road. He wore a face mask, its red eyes gleaming through the storm. When he reached the edge of a ruined city, he pulled out a handheld device with a rectangular lens that glowed a bright blue.

He tried to activate it, but it sputtered and turned itself off. He shook it and tapped it, and it popped back to life, shooting out a bright field of blue light against the rain. The pilot swept the cone back and forth across the ruin, and dozens of

9

blue pinpoints glowed along the devastated city's edge. Then the holo-mapping device fed those dots into its processor and created a hologram of what the city had looked like during its last days before the planet had destroyed it. Grainy projections of streets and buildings hung in the air, glowing red ghosts of a great city now centuries gone.

In front of the pilot snaked a road that led directly to a building near the edge of the hologram projection. On that building a tracking beacon lit up. It looked like a target, and that's exactly what it was: the target of this expedition.

The pilot followed the road, passing through the hologram ghosts of Morag's citizens. People went about their business. A little girl played with a dog. The pilot was a little surprised to learn that Morag's inhabitants had been human.

He reached the ruined building and stepped inside, getting out of the rain. The wind still blew, but not nearly as hard in the enclosed space. Part of the roof had fallen in, and shafts of dim light shone down onto the rubble-strewn floor. The interior of the building was large, with thirty-foot ceilings and pillars supporting them. The pilot looked over the scene, and when he seemed satisfied that he was safe, he touched the side of his mask.

With a crackle, it disappeared, leaving only an earpiece, and Peter Quill got down to business.

The first thing he did was put on his headphones and crank up Awesome Mix Tape Vol. 1. He couldn't do anything without his music. Then he started to tap one foot, and pretty soon he was dancing, grooving his way through the ruin and into an open plaza beyond. The rain had stopped, and he kept right on jamming, moving across the open plaza to the familiar rhythms of the songs that had kept him company for twenty-six years. He splashed through mud puddles, chased away a small pack of aggressive little lizardlike animals, and reached the edge of a huge crack in the ground. Still keeping the rhythm, he fired up the rockets in his boots and spanned the gap in a long, rocket-assisted step. On the other side, he came to a sealed door. He inserted a key into the lock, which spun with a squeal. The door opened, revealing a smaller chamber with a glowing blue containment tube sitting on a pedestal at its center.

He took a transparent globe out of his coat pocket. When he shook it, bright light glowed from within, illuminating the room. He was alone. Good. He set the globe down and unhooked a triangular metal device from his belt.

In the years since he was abducted from Earth, Peter had seen a lot. He'd seen a planet made of fire with a moon made of ice. He'd seen an army of shape-shifting aliens attack a space whale. He'd even watched as twin suns went supernova together. It had been a pretty amazing couple of decades.

He'd worked his way through the ranks on the Ravager outlaw ship that had picked him up. He had started as the space equivalent of a deckhand and risen all the way to being his captain's second in command. It was a pretty good life. Lots of adventure, always something new to see and do...but in all these years, there was one thing he'd never been. He'd never been rich.

If things worked out here in the ruins of this ancient Morag temple, though, that would change.

Inside the glowing blue containment field was a metallic Orb, its surface carved in a complex pattern. Peter had done a little research—well, more than a little—on this item, and although he didn't know exactly what it was, he knew a couple of things about it.

One, the Broker would pay him a lot of money for it.

Two, it was well protected. The containment field would pretty much disintegrate anything that touched it from the outside, and he didn't know how to turn it off. So he'd flipped the problem on its head and decided that if he couldn't reach in and get it, he'd just have to convince the Orb to come out on its own.

That was where the triangular device came into play. It was designed to electromagnetically attract certain kinds of metal alloys, and the Orb was made of just such an alloy. Beyond that, Peter had no idea what it was for. He didn't care, either. He just knew the Orb would make him rich, so he had come to Morag to get it.

He turned on the attractor. It snapped into an open position, with three sides of the pyramid turning into legs that braced it on the floor. The fourth side was the electromagnetic field generator. It started to hum.

Inside the containment field, the Orb moved. It pressed slowly through the containment field, shedding tendrils of plasma as it pushed through each layer. Peter watched, ready to make a break for a good hiding place if there was another layer of security he hadn't noticed. You saw all kinds of weird things in these old ruins. His time with the Ravagers had taught him that, along with a lot of other things.

Nothing went wrong, though. The Orb slowly emerged through the outer layer of the containment field, then popped free and floated down to clink into place on the attractor. Behind it, the containment field went dark.

"Ha-ha!" Peter shouted happily as he turned off the attractor and picked up the Orb. He was so happy to have his hands on the artifact that he wanted to kiss it, and he might have done just that...except that was when he heard an all-too-familiar voice growl, "Drop it!"

Oops. He wasn't alone after all.

Peter spun to see the Sakaaran mercenary known as Korath, flanked by several of his favorite goons. All of them held weapons leveled at him. They were big and bad—especially Korath, who had some kind of machine grafted into his skull that amped up his strength and reflexes. They had him at a real disadvantage. The solution? Play it cool.

"Uh, hey," he said, trying to keep his voice even.

"Drop it now!" Korath shouted. The other Sakaarans were shouting, too, but they didn't speak English and Peter didn't know any Sakaaran, so he didn't worry about what they were saying.

"Hey, cool, man, no problem." Peter let the Orb fall to the floor and roll until it clinked up against a stone block fallen from the roof. "No problem at all."

Korath picked up the Orb and brandished it at Peter. "How did you know about this?"

"I don't even know what that is! I'm just a junker, man," explained Peter. "I was just checking stuff out."

Korath took a moment to look Peter over from top to

14

bottom. Peter had a bad feeling about what he was going to say next.

"You don't look like a junker," Korath grunted. "You're wearing Ravager gear."

That was the problem with uniforms. The Ravagers were a gang of criminals that pulled off jobs in this sector, and if you crossed them, you usually weren't heard from again. Peter was, in fact, a Ravager, wearing Ravager gear. He'd been hoping Korath and the Sakaarans wouldn't recognize it.

"You better stop poking me," Peter growled at one of the mercenaries who kept prodding him with a gun every time Korath spoke.

"What is your name?" Korath demanded.

"My name is Peter Quill, okay? Dude, chill out."

"Move!" Korath commanded. His soldiers echoed the command in Sakaaran, shoving at Peter.

"Why?"

"Ronan might have some questions for you."

Ronan. That was bad news. Peter didn't know a lot about Ronan, but what he did know made him want to steer way clear. Like light-years away. Ronan was Kree, and angry, and had a tendency to kill a lot of people. Peter did not want to be in a position where Ronan was asking him questions.

What the heck, he thought. They know about the Ravagers. No point in keeping any other secrets.

"Hey, you know what?" Peter asked. "There is another name you might know me by..."

Korath paused in the temple doorway. "What is that?"

Peter looked him right in the eyes and prepared to enjoy the impact his revelation would make. "Star-Lord," he said.

Korath looked confused. "Who?"

"Star-Lord, man!" Peter couldn't believe Korath hadn't heard of him. Didn't he have any kind of reputation? "The legendary outlaw!" he added, hoping to prod Korath's memory...and also he was already starting to formulate the outlines of a plan.

Korath spread his arms, looking confused. His soldiers muttered among themselves. Peter turned to them. "Guys?"

They just stared at him.

Korath lost interest and ran out of patience at the same time. "Move!" he commanded again, with a gesture toward the door.

"Ahh, forget this," Peter said. What did a guy have to do to get a little galactic notoriety?

Right at the moment when the Sakaarans had completely fallen for his wounded-pride act, Peter kicked the glowing globe into the soldiers' midst. It shattered, splashing hot white plasma over them.

They screamed and thrashed as Peter drew his blasters and dropped Korath just as he was turning around in the doorway. The Orb bounced out of Korath's hand and Peter picked it up. He took a moment to savor the success of his ruse. The Sakaarans had been completely fooled!

Although, he admitted to himself, he was a little irritated that they hadn't known who he was.

He heard a moan from the doorway and looked up just as Korath staggered to his feet and leveled his rifle at Peter.

The energy bolt from the rifle would have disintegrated most of Peter's torso... if he hadn't thrown himself straight down onto the floor, landing hard enough to knock the wind out of him. Instead it blew a five-foot hole in the wall behind Peter.

Hey, he thought. *An emergency exit!*

He triggered his boots' rocket thrusters and blasted out through the hole as a second shot from Korath hit the edge of the hole. That got him a head start, but Peter's problems weren't over yet. The boot thrusters were designed to fire against the ground. When they shot him out at a shallow angle through the hole in the temple wall, he completely lost his equilibrium and ended up crashing hard on the wet, rocky ground outside.

Peter scrambled to his feet and ran for his ship. Korath had gotten to the hole in the wall, screaming at the top of his lungs. Peter glanced back and saw the Sakaaran commander leap an incredible distance after him. *Yikes*, he thought, and ran faster. If he could get to the ship before Korath…

Uh-oh. Peter skidded to a halt, seeing five more Sakaarans standing guard between him and his ship, the good old *Milano*, built along the lines of a bird of prey, with a sharp nose and hooked wings that gave it maneuverability in atmospheres but also kept its engines mounted far apart for nimble piloting in space. She was a beauty, and clearly Korath had spotted her on the way in. He was no dummy. He'd made sure he had a backup plan.

But hey, so had Peter. Sort of. In fact, he'd just thought of it! He saw that the Sakaaran mercenaries wore metallic armor, and he started running again. Toward them.

They shouted and raised their rifles, but before they could draw a bead on him Peter threw the attractor into their midst. It glowed and powered up, and in a split second they crashed together over it, held fast by the immense power of its electromagnetic field.

A geyser erupted in the shattered landscape as Peter

jumped past the magnetically stuck Sakaarans. Another blast from Korath's rifle sizzled through the rain, which was falling harder again. While he was in the air, Peter hit the control that opened the *Milano*'s cockpit. He landed at the base of one wing and skidded through the open hatch, landing a lot harder than he'd meant to.

With a groan he sat up and started closing the hatch. While he got the engines fired up, Korath's pals finally broke the hold of the attractor and stood up. With Korath shouting over them, they started to set up some kind of heavy mounted gun. Peter knew he did not want to be around when it was ready.

He got off the ground and rolled the ship hard to the right as Korath's crew fired the first shot from their cannon. It crackled under the wing and destroyed a rocky spire. Peter hauled the *Milano* around in a tight turn and wound its main thrusters all the way up. More blasts from Korath's cannon tore through the storm as Peter accelerated out of range, laughing like he'd just won the lottery. Which he sort of had! Escaping from a dozen Sakaaran soldiers with a lost treasure he'd dug out of a Moragian tomb—man, if that didn't add to the legend of "Star-Lord the Outlaw," nothing would.

But he'd started congratulating himself a little too soon. A huge geyser, maybe ten thousand times the size of the one that he'd run past a minute before, erupted straight under the *Milano* and snuffed out the ship's engines. *Ah, geez,* Peter thought. In atmospheres he had to use air intakes, and the geyser had turned them into water intakes.

The *Milano* tumbled and spun back toward the surface. Peter bounced and rolled around its spacious cockpit, wishing he'd had a chance to buckle his seat belt. Everything he'd had in his backpack, way back when, was flying around. Peter strained to reach the lever that would vent the intakes and restart the engines. Escaping Sakaarans wouldn't do him any good if he smashed himself to pieces on the rocks.

Man, those rocks were getting closer fast. Peter strained a little harder... and got a hand on the lever. He blew the vents and also used the lever to pull himself back into the pilot's chair. With maybe fifty yards to spare, he got the engines fired up again and the *Milano* stabilized and hovered, rocking in the storm but well away from Korath and his goons.

He got his breath, got his bearings, and got away from Morag as fast as he could.

Hours later, with the ship set on course for the planet Xandar, where he would meet the Broker, Peter sat in his pilot chair idly tossing the Orb into the air and catching it, the way he once had with a baseball when he was a kid. He was rocking out to Awesome Mix Tape Vol. 1, which played in a stereo tape deck he'd had custom-made on Xandar a few years before. He'd shown the guy the tape, explained how it worked—at least as far as he knew—and now the *Milano* was a spacefaring concert hall. Peter was daydreaming of all the things he would do when the Orb had made him rich and watching the holo-news. The Kree Empire was in an uproar over a peace treaty the emperor had signed with Xandar—and by extension, Nova Prime, the leader of the Nova Corps. They were the law in this part of the galaxy, a cadre of take-no-prisoners tough guys who also were about the only thing keeping the Kree in check.

Peter was considering the situation, hoping things would stay calm on Xandar long enough for him to make the deal for the Orb, when a video call interrupted the holo-feed.

It was Yondu, the leader of the Ravagers and the person responsible for kidnapping Peter from Earth...and, he had to admit, for more or less raising him afterward. He was a humanoid, with blue skin, a Mohawk-shaped steel ridge on his skull, and anger management issues.

"Quill!" Yondu yelled. He was almost always yelling.

"Hey, Yondu," Peter said casually.

"I'm here on Morag. Ain't no Orb, ain't no you."

"Yeah, I was in the neighborhood. I thought I'd save you the hassle," Peter said. He had to keep Yondu talking for a minute while he figured out how to handle the situation. The thing was, Peter wasn't supposed to have gone to Morag. The Ravagers—meaning Yondu—had cut the original deal with the Broker, and Peter had decided it seemed like a good opportunity to strike out on his own.

Problem was, Yondu wasn't going to see it that way.

Yondu's eyes narrowed. "Well, where you at now, boy?" he demanded.

"I feel really bad about this, but I'm not going to tell you that."

Yondu's face twisted in anger. "I slaved making this deal!"

"'Slaved'?" Peter echoed.

Yondu kept right on talking—well, shouting—over him. "And now you're going to rip me off?"

"Making a few calls is 'slaved'? I mean, really?"

Yondu's eyes looked like they were about to pop out of his blue face. "We do not do that to each other. We're Ravagers. We got a code!"

"Yeah, and that code is: Steal from everybody," Peter reminded him. It's exactly what Yondu had told him when Peter was being initiated into the Ravagers.

"When I picked you up from Terra, these boys of mine wanted to eat you!"

Picked me up, Peter thought. Funny way of saying "kidnapped."

"Yeah?"

"They never tasted any Terran before. I stopped them! You're alive because of me! I will find you!"

Peter made a slashing gesture with his hand to cut off the call. As he did, he heard Yondu turning to the other Ravagers and growling, "Put a bounty on him!"

A bounty. Whatever. It probably wasn't the only one. Peter relaxed in his ship, regarding the Orb and once again dreaming up ways to spend his money. It wouldn't be long before he got to Xandar.

Furious, Yondu turned to his Ravagers. "Forty K!" he said, meaning a bounty of forty thousand units. "But I want him alive!"

"Alive?" repeated Horuz, his lieutenant and old friend.

"That's what I said." Yondu stomped back toward the Ravager ship.

"I told you when we picked that kid up you should have delivered him like we was hired to do!" Horuz raged as he followed Yondu. "He was cargo! You have always been soft on him!"

Yondu turned to face Horuz. "You're the only one I'm being soft on!" he yelled, flipping open his coat to reveal the foot-long arrow attached to his belt. Horuz froze. The arrow glowed red-hot, and Yondu could telepathically control it. A thought from him would send it flying to strike any target…including Horuz's head.

"Now don't you worry about Mr. Quill," Yondu said in a lower tone of voice. "Soon as we get him back here, I'm gonna kill him myself. What we do need to worry about is who else out there wants that Orb."

CHAPTER 2

anging in the blackness of space, the *Dark Aster* looked like a cross between a battle cruiser and a fortress. Wherever the warship appeared, it brought fear. Whole planets had been evacuated based only on rumors the *Dark Aster* was approaching.

It wasn't so feared because it was one of the most heavily armed warships ever created—which it was—but because it was the flagship of none other than Ronan. Some knew him as "Ronan the Murderer"; others as "Ronan the Butcher"; and still others as "Ronan the Warlord." All these names were meant to slur Ronan for his cruelty and heartlessness—but they pleased him, and there was one name he preferred above all the others: "Ronan the Accuser." Ronan looked upon the people of this galaxy and accused them of the greatest crime he could imagine—weakness.

Ronan was Kree, a member of an empire that had once dominated huge sections of the galaxy. He was tall and incredibly strong and dwarfed those around him. He was the perfect specimen even among the immensely powerful Kree, strong in body and in mind. His will was unchangeable, his principles absolute.

"They call me terrorist, radical, zealot, because I obey the ancient laws of my people, the Kree, and punish those who do not." Ronan spoke as he rose from a cleansing pool of midnight-black fluid. His attendants gathered around him to anoint his body with sacred powders and apply the mask of the Accuser to his face. "Because I do not forgive your people for taking the life of my father. And his father, and his father before him. A thousand years of war between us will not be forgotten!"

This speech was addressed to a prisoner, who knelt in the chamber, his upper body immobilized by a heavy steel collar around his neck. He could barely turn his head. The prisoner was an officer of the Nova Corps, the

26

Xandar-based law enforcement agency that policed the sector. Fully dressed in his armor and the cowl of his office, Ronan turned to face the prisoner, who glared defiantly up at him.

"You can't do this! Our government signed a peace treaty!" he protested.

Ronan despised the Nova Corps because they represented everything he hated about Xandarian civilization. The weakness, the cowardly use of diplomacy to avoid the righteous fury of war. The Nova Corps' vision of law was nothing more than saving the weak from their own weakness. They were a sickness.

"My government knows no shame," Ronan said. "The Xandarians and your culture are a disease." He held out his hand and one of his attendants gave him the Cosmi-Rod, a hammer more than a meter long that channeled Ronan's power and was also the symbol of his Accuser status. The government of the Kree might not recognize him, but Kree tradition did—and Ronan cared more for tradition than for government.

"You will never rule Xandar," the officer said.

"No," Ronan said. "I will cure it!"

He brought the hammer down, and the galaxy was one step closer to being free of the Nova Corps' disease.

Nebula, daughter of Thanos, had been waiting in the shadows while her associate administered justice. "Ronan," she said now, "Korath has returned."

Ronan met the Sakaaran in the *Dark Aster*'s throne room, flanked by statues of the Accusers who had come before him. Also present were Nebula and Gamora, another of Thanos's daughters. Both of them were on the *Dark Aster* as Thanos's representatives and watchdogs over Ronan. He resented the fact that Thanos chose to keep watch over him, but there was nothing he could do about it.

Both Nebula and Gamora were pitiless assassins, who would do whatever Thanos commanded—and whatever Ronan commanded, as long as it agreed with their orders from their father. He listened as Korath reported his failure to obtain the Orb due to the interference of another.

"Master, he is a thief, an outlaw who calls himself Star-Lord," Korath said. "But we have discovered he has an agreement to retrieve the Orb for an intermediary known as the Broker."

"I promised Thanos I would retrieve the Orb for him," Ronan murmured. "Only then will he destroy Xandar for me."

He stood. "Nebula, go to Xandar and get me the Orb."

"It will be my honor," she said.

Stepping forward, Gamora said, "It will be your doom. If this happens again, you'll be facing our father without his prize."

"I'm a daughter of Thanos, just like you," Nebula said. Ronan saw she was getting angry. *Good*, he thought. Let them hate each other. Then they will pay less attention to me.

"But I know Xandar," Gamora said.

Nebula's tone grew sharper. "Ronan has already decreed that I—"

"Do not speak for me," Ronan commanded. He had to suffer the presence of Thanos's daughters, but he insisted they would answer to him while they were on his ship.

He stepped up to Gamora and whispered, "You will not fail."

Nebula watched, both furious at being passed over and smirking at her sister in the focus of Ronan's unnerving gaze.

But Gamora looked Ronan right in the eye and said, "Have I ever?"

CHAPTER 3

It was a great day at the mall. The Xandarian sun was shining, the air was warm, and people were out having a good time. There were families playing, shoppers scoring deals, friends dining outside at the mall's many fine restaurants—and Rocket had nothing but scorn for all of it.

"Xandarians," he grumbled. He surveyed the crowds through a scope, doing a face scan and comparing everyone he saw to a database of outstanding bounties. Only certain people knew about that database, and Rocket was one of them. He liked bounty hunting. It had lots of variety, there was lots of shooting, and the money was tip-top.

He hid in the bushes at the edge of a balcony overlooking the swanky mall plaza below. You could find people with bounties on their heads anywhere, but the high-value marks had a tendency to try to blend in with fancy surroundings. If you wanted to load up on five-hundred-unit lowlifes, there were places for that, but those guys weren't worth Rocket's time. He and Groot were after the big score.

He stood up on tiptoes to get a better look at the areas right below him. Rocket was barely three feet tall, and looked like a cute and cuddly mammal, like you might find begging for treats in a Xandarian family's kitchen. Except as far as he knew there was nothing like him anywhere in the galaxy, and he was not cuddly. No, sir. Rocket liked flying ships real fast, and shooting guns real loud, and breaking any law he ran across.

"What a bunch of losers. All of 'em, in a big hurry to get from stupid to nothing at all. Pathetic," said Rocket, his upper lip curling in disgust.

His scope landed on an average-looking human, strolling by himself. "Look at this guy! You believe they call us criminals when he's assaulting us with that haircut?"

Groot didn't answer, but then, Groot didn't talk much. He was an eight-foot-tall walking tree, more or less, so talking wasn't his strong suit. What Groot was good at was fighting and growing pieces of himself back when they got blown off. Plus he was as strong as any living being Rocket had ever known, which came in handy given Rocket's own compact stature.

Next, Rocket scoped a tiny human stumbling along the sidewalk holding the hands of an adult. "What is this thing? It thinks it's so cool. It's not cool to get help! Walk by yourself, you little gargoyle."

He moved on to an older human, clearly trying to get the interest of a much younger female. "Look at Mr. Smiles over here. Where's your wife, old man? Ha! Right, Groot?"

Rocket laughed, getting a kick out of himself. He turned to see if Groot had seen the old guy, and noticed that Groot wasn't paying attention at all. He was leaning over a nearby fountain and watering his insides. In other words, drinking.

"Don't drink fountain water, you idiot! That's disgusting!" Rocket shouted.

Groot stood up and shook his head, grunting.

"Yes, you did! I just saw you doing it. Why are you lying?"

His scope's alarm went off, notifying Rocket that he'd accidentally waved it so that it focused on someone carrying a bounty. "Oh, looks like we got one," he said. He looked at the target. "Okay, humie," he said. That was his preferred insulting term for humans. "How bad does someone want to find you?"

The display on the scope identified the humie in question as Peter Quill...and the bounty as more than Rocket would have expected. A lot more. "Forty thousand units? Groot, we're gonna be rich."

He turned to see Groot drinking from the fountain again, completely oblivious to this huge potential score. Rocket sighed. Some people.

Peter walked from the mall's main thoroughfare up to the Broker's pawnshop. There was no sign, but the door knew Peter from a previous visit and opened automatically at his approach. The Broker had very good security, and he needed it. He dealt with items that were highly sought after.

"Mr. Quill," the Broker said when he saw Peter enter. He was a smallish humanoid, with ridges on his bare scalp. Hair grew between them but nowhere else on his head except for his eyebrows, which were like small wings swooping over his forehead. He was dressed, as always, in a suit that cost more than all of the clothes Peter had bought in his whole life. Total.

"Broker," Peter said. Getting down to business, he plunked the Orb down on the Broker's desk. "The Orb. As commissioned."

The Broker regarded him with suspicion. "Where is Yondu?"

"Wanted to be here," Peter said. "Sends his love, and told me to tell you that you got the best eyebrows in the business."

The Broker sniffed, dismissing the humorous compliment. He picked up the Orb and set it aside. "What is it?" Peter asked.

"It's my policy never to discuss my clients, or their needs," the Broker said.

"Yeah, well, I almost died getting it for you."

Unfazed, the Broker said, "An occupational hazard, I'm sure, in your line of work."

"Some machine-headed freak," Peter said, describing Korath as he continued his story, "working for a dude named Ronan."

The name had a startling effect on the Broker. "Ronan?" Immediately he came around his desk and began ushering

Peter toward the door. "I'm sorry, Mr. Quill, I truly am, but I want no part of this transaction if Ronan is involved!" He slapped the Orb back into Peter's hands.

"Whoa, whoa! Who's Ronan?" Peter asked. The Broker kept pushing him toward the door.

"A Kree fanatic, outraged by the peace treaty, who will not rest until Xandarian culture—my culture!—is wiped from existence!" He had pushed Peter most of the way to the door by now.

"Come on," Peter said.

"He's someone whose bad side I'd rather not be on," the Broker said. Clearly he was terrified of this Ronan, and Peter couldn't figure it out. He'd never heard of the guy.

"What about my bad side?" he joked, trying to lighten things up a little.

"Farewell, Mr. Quill!" the Broker shouted. He waved to open his door and shoved Peter out.

The moment Peter's body crossed the threshold, the door hissed shut. "Hey, we had a deal, bro!" Peter shouted through the door.

No answer.

He stood there fuming. How was he going to get rich now? Yondu was after him, this Ronan guy seemed like bad news...man, everything was getting complicated.

35

To one side of the door, a beautiful woman with green skin and long dark hair reddened at the tips was delicately eating a piece of fruit. She was looking at Peter, so he tried to get himself together. He didn't like losing his temper in front of good-looking women.

"What happened?" she asked.

"This guy just backed out of a deal on me," Peter groused. "If there's one thing I hate, it's a man without integrity."

She watched, finishing her fruit. She looked mighty fine in her black leather jumpsuit, and the knives on her hips gave her a nice little air of menace. "Peter Quill," Peter said, introducing himself. "People call me Star-Lord."

"You have the bearing of a man of honor," she said.

"Well, you know, I wouldn't say that," said Peter, playing humble. "People say it about me, but it's not something I would ever say about myself."

As he finished the sentence, she was walking closer to him, and he was enjoying her walking closer to him. Then, almost faster than he could follow, she snatched the Orb from his hands, doubled him over with a kick to the stomach, and ran.

Peter stood up, out of breath. There was no way he would catch her in a footrace. She was fast. Luckily he had a little electronic bolo in his pocket that he kept for circumstances like this one. He activated it and slung it sidearm after her.

The bolo spun through the air past startled shoppers and wrapped itself several times around the woman's knees, bringing her down.

Peter was on her in a second, running and leaping to get hold of her before she could untangle the bolo and get away again. She met him in midair with both feet, kicking him hard off to the side. He hit the pavement, the wind knocked out of him for the second time in fifteen seconds. Before he could get up, she was pounding him with fists, elbows, and feet—all without getting up herself! Even though he was getting beaten senseless, Peter couldn't help but admire her technique.

She straddled him, a look of regret on her face. "This wasn't the plan," she said, and drew one of those knives he'd noticed earlier.

But before she could use it, a tiny ball of fur came flying out of nowhere and knocked her over sideways. She cried out as she hit the pavement and Peter saw what looked like—no, it couldn't be...

It was. A talking raccoon. Big one, maybe three feet tall.

"Put him in the bag!" the raccoon was shouting. The green woman got back to her feet and tried to pull it off, but it hung on for dear life.

Peter looked around. Put who in the bag? Then he saw the walking tree holding a giant sack. It started extruding roots from its body, wrapping them around the green woman.

"Not her—him!" the raccoon shouted. "Learn genders, man!" He was grappling with the green woman's head, and one of his paws slipped into her mouth. She bit him, hard. "Biting? That's not fair!"

Peter happened to agree—biting was not cool—but he wasn't going to stick around and argue about it. Whoever the raccoon and tree were, whatever was happening, he had a chance to get out. He grabbed the Orb and ran, glancing over his shoulder to track their pursuit.

Screaming in fury, the green woman tore the raccoon free and flung him down into the lower level of the plaza. He slammed into a transparent wall and landed in a heap. Peter turned away to gain speed, and a moment later the Orb was knocked out of his hand with a sharp metallic ping. He looked down and saw it rolling away. He also saw a small throwing knife clattering to the pavement.

She'd thrown a knife at him! But not to kill him. Interesting, he thought. She likes me.

But she seemed to like the Orb more. She jumped over the balcony and ran for the Orb. Peter ran along the balcony as she picked up the Orb, waiting for the right time…now!

He vaulted over and landed on her, driving her to the ground. But she was a lot quicker than he was, and stronger, too. In a moment she had him flipped on his back with one knee pressed hard under his chin.

"Fool," she said. "You should have learned."

"I don't learn," Peter admitted. "One of my issues."

She gave him a look and, just for a second, forgot to stab him. He took the momentary opportunity to slap one of his boot rockets onto her hip and fire it up.

It shot her away over the plaza to land in a shallow reflecting pool. She skidded all the way across the pool, kicking up a big rooster tail along the way and smashing hard into the wall on the other side. The crowd gasped. They hadn't come to the mall for a show like this.

Peter stood, thinking the show was over…and that's when the tree got the drop on him and stuffed him into a sack.

The job was getting complicated, Rocket thought. He hated complicated jobs.

The target was yelling inside the bag, the green woman was nowhere to be found, the Xandarian law would show up any minute…and Groot was strolling along with the bag over his shoulder and a grin on his face, like he didn't have a care in the world.

"Quit smiling, you idiot," Rocket grumbled. "You're supposed to be a professional."

Then he turned around just in time for the green woman to shove him out of the way. "You gotta be kidding me— Hey!"

Without saying a word, she walked up to Groot with a sword in her hand and started hacking.

Groot was tough, but he was also surprised. She came at him faster than he could block—and when he did block, she hacked off first one arm and then the other. Then, while he was looking down at himself in amazement, she turned around and opened the bag holding the humie target. Whatshisname, Peter Quill. It was all over in seconds, before Rocket could even draw a gun.

But when she opened the sack, there was Quill pointing a gun at her.

It went off with a crackle and a blue flash, and the green woman went over flat on her back, twitching as the stun current arced and sizzled over her body. The target was up and running. Groot didn't have any arms, and he wasn't that fast regardless.

It was time to take decisive action. "I live for the simple things," Rocket said as he shouldered a four-barreled rifle almost as long as he was tall. "Like how much this is gonna hurt." He got Peter Quill in his sights and fired.

A globe of blue energy, similar to what Quill had used to zap Gamora, blazed across the plaza and hit Quill square between the shoulder blades. He went down and started yelling and twitching. "Yeah," Rocket chuckled. "Writhe, little man."

Served him right for making the job so complicated.

Off to his left, Groot was making whimpering noises and prodding his severed arms with one foot. "It'll grow back, ya daft idiot," Rocket said. "Quit whining." Like it was the first time Groot had lost a limb, he thought. Yeesh. They always grew back.

He started to walk over to where Quill was still jerking around on the ground, but his foot wouldn't touch the ground—and a moment later, Rocket realized he was in the grip of a Nova Corps stasis beam. It had him hanging a few feet in the air. Groot, too. Probably the green woman and Quill, but he couldn't see them.

He could, however, turn his head enough to see that

the mall plaza was encircled by Nova Corps light fighter craft.

"Subject 89P13," one of the pilots said over a loudspeaker. "Drop your weapon."

"Aw, crap," Rocket said. He let the rifle go.

"By order of the Nova Corps, you are all under arrest for endangerment to life and damage of property," the pilot continued.

Floating around in the stasis beam, Rocket saw that other Nova Corps officers were helping Quill to his feet. "Hey!" one of them said. "If it isn't Star-Prince."

Quill rolled his eyes. "Lord."

One of the other soldiers laughed.

"I picked this guy up for petty theft. He's got a code name," the officer said, mocking Quill a little more.

"Come on, man," Quill said. "It's an outlaw name."

"Just relax, pal," the officer said. "It's cool to have a code name. It's not that weird."

They walked Quill away as Rocket, Groot, and the green woman rose higher in the air. "Fascists," Rocket spat.

CHAPTER 4

"Ronan is destroying Xandarian outposts throughout the galaxy," Nova Prime was arguing from her top-floor office at the headquarters of the Nova Corps. She was a human in late middle age, with a record of skill and resolve in handling diplomatic problems, but the Kree were frustrating her. She tried not to show how angry she was at their refusal to do anything about Ronan's attacks. "I should think that would call for some slight response on the part of the Kree."

"We signed your peace treaty, Nova Prime," the Kree ambassador replied. "What more do you want?"

"At least a statement from the Kree Empire saying that they condemn his actions. He is slaughtering children. Families."

"That is your business," the ambassador said. "Now I have other matters to attend to." He pinched his fingers shut, closing the video link without even pretending to be polite.

Nova Prime muttered something extremely impolite and turned to see one of her officers approaching. "Well, there's some good news," he said. "It looks like we've apprehended one of Ronan's compatriots."

Many floors below, in the Nova Corps inmate processing center, Corpsman Dey—who had helped Peter Quill to his feet an hour before—was identifying and cataloguing the new prisoners. "Gamora," he read from a display, as the green woman stood impassively in a holding area. "Surgically modified and trained as a living weapon. The adopted daughter of the Mad Titan, Thanos. Recently Thanos lent her and her sister, Nebula, out to Ronan, which leads us to believe that Thanos and Ronan are working together."

Dey moved on. "Subject 89P13 calls itself Rocket," he said. "The result of illegal genetic and cybernetic experiments on a lower life-form."

Rocket spat on the floor.

Dey cycled to the next new prisoner. Behind him, his superior officer, Saal, was startled by the sight. "What the—?"

"They call it Groot," Dey said. "A humanoid plant that's been traveling recently as 89P13's personal houseplant-slash-muscle." The huge treelike being's arms were beginning to regenerate, Dey noticed. It would probably be back to normal by the next day.

Then he came to the last of them. "Peter Jason Quill, from Terra." In the holding cell, Quill was making a rude gesture. "Raised from youth by a band of mercenaries called the Ravagers, led by Yondu Udonta."

Pursing his lips, Saal said, "Transport all four to the Kyln."

Floating in the midst of an asteroid field that was the remains of a destroyed planet, the Kyln was a space station prison on the remote edge of the Xandarian sphere of influence.

From the outside, it looked like an ordinary station, perhaps supporting asteroid mining or research. But its inside was crammed with some of the most hard-core criminals that sector of the galaxy had ever known.

"I guess most of Nova Corps want to uphold the laws," Rocket was saying as he, Groot, Gamora, and Peter were processed into the Kyln. "But these ones here? They're corrupt and cruel. But hey," he added with a chuckle, "that's not my problem. I ain't gonna be here long. I've escaped twenty-two prisons. This one's no different." Rocket glanced over his shoulder at Peter. "You're lucky Gamora here showed up, otherwise me and Groot'd be collecting that bounty right now, and you'd be getting drawn and quartered by Yondu and those Ravagers."

"I've had a lot of folks try to kill me over the years, and I ain't about to be brought down by a tree and a talking raccoon," Peter shot back.

"What's a raccoon?" asked Rocket, like it might be an insult he'd never heard.

"What's a raccoon? It's what you are, stupid."

"Ain't no thing like me, 'cept me," huffed Rocket indignantly.

"So this Orb has a real shiny blue suitcase, Ark of the Covenant sort of vibe," Peter said to Gamora. "What is it?"

"I am Groot," Groot said.

"So what?" Peter snapped. He repeated his question to Gamora. "What's the Orb?"

"I have no words for an honorless thief," said Gamora, not even bothering to look at Peter.

"Pretty high and mighty coming from the lackey of a genocidal maniac," Rocket responded. Gamora turned and glared at him, but he continued defiantly and she looked away again. "Yeah, I know who you are. Anyone who's anyone knows who you are."

"Yeah, we know who you are!" Peter confirmed, but then he turned and quietly whispered to Groot. "Who is she again?"

"I am Groot," Groot whispered back.

Peter rolled his eyes. "Yeah. You said that."

"I wasn't retrieving the Orb for Ronan," Gamora said. "I was betraying him. I had an agreement to sell it to a third party."

Ahead of them, the lead guard in their escort keyed a code into a panel cybernetically wired into his forearm. Peter saw Rocket watching him and wondered why.

"I am Groot," said Groot.

"Well, that's just as fascinating as the first eighty-nine times you told me that," Peter said, with all the sarcasm he could muster. Which was a lot. "What is wrong with the tree here?"

They went through a security portal and into a hallway leading deeper into the Kyln.

"Well, he don't know talking good like me and you," Rocket explained. "His vocabulistics are limited to 'I' and 'am' and 'Groot,' exclusively in that order."

"Well, I tell you what, that's going to wear real thin real fast," Peter said. Then he heard something.

Music.

His music.

It was playing from a workbench in a storage area off the passage, and when Peter followed the sound, he saw one of the prison guards playing his music through his headphones from his tape player.

And he lost it.

"Hey!" he called out. "Put that away!"

The guard put the headphones on and Peter ducked through the open doorway. An alarm chirped and the door closed behind him. "Hey!" he said again. "Listen to me, you big blue bastard, take those headphones off. That's mine. Those belong to impound." Prisoners didn't get to keep their personal belongings, but they were supposed to be stored securely, not picked over by thieving guards. The guard took the headphones off and stared Peter down.

"That tape and that player are mine!" Peter shouted, and that's when the guard had had enough.

He came around the workbench and hit Peter with a stun baton that shot electricity through his body, doubling him over in pain. He screamed and hit the floor, but kept himself from collapsing completely. "That song belongs to me!"

It was all he had left from Earth. All he had left from his mother. Awesome Mix Tape Vol. 1 was his last link to the boy he had been before the Ravagers took him.

The guard hit him with the baton again. Peter went down, and the guard hit him again. He didn't remember anything for a while after that.

He recovered soon enough, but Peter's usual upbeat mood was shattered. He couldn't lose Awesome Mix Tape Vol. 1. Prison didn't scare him, but that did. The group was processed, given uniforms to wear, and escorted into the main yard. The whole time they were watched by auto-mated floating drones that threatened to attack them if they stepped out of line. While they were getting dressed in their yellow prison clothes, Peter saw scars and crude cybernetic implants all up and down Rocket's back. He didn't say anything, but he felt a surge of sympathy for the obnoxious little animal. Everyone had a history, and Rocket's had been especially cruel to him.

But at least Groot's arms had grown all the way back.

The prison floors were circular, ringing a common area where prisoners played cards, talked, fought, and otherwise lived their lives under the watchful eye of the drones—and of a prison guard up in a central tower, who could see the entire area from his station. When Peter and the group emerged, the inmates started shouting and threatening them. Some threw things. A piece of some unidentifiable prison food hit Peter and he flinched.

At first Peter thought the prisoners were trying to hit him. Then he realized they were shouting *Murderer!...* and then he realized they were shouting it at Gamora. "Coming for you first, Gamora!" he heard one of them scream. "You're dead!"

Peter looked at Rocket in confusion.

"It's like I said." Rocket shrugged. "She's got a rep. A lot of prisoners here have lost their families to Ronan and his goons. She'll last a day, tops."

"No... The guards will protect her, right?" asked Peter.

Rocket laughed darkly at this. "They're here to stop us from getting out. They don't care what we do to each other inside."

Peter looked at Gamora, seeing that she had heard everything Rocket said. She looked resolute. "Whatever nightmares the future holds," she said to both Rocket and Peter, "are dreams compared to what's behind me."

Peter hoped Rocket was wrong...but in another moment he had his own problems, as a giant blue monster, barely humanoid, blocked his way. "Check out the new meat," it said, and would have gone farther but Groot stepped up and extended two roots from his hand. The blue monstrosity didn't register them as a threat until it was too late, and the roots were already growing into its nose. It cried out in pain as Groot lifted it from the floor. Peter was astonished. It must have weighed three hundred pounds, easy, and Groot didn't seem to be straining at all.

The rest of the inmates stopped what they were doing to watch the show, and Rocket took full advantage. He stepped out into the space cleared around Groot and pointed at Peter. "Let's make something clear!" he called out over the blue creature's groans. "This one here is our booty! You wanna get to him, you go through us! Or, more accurately...we go through you."

With a crunch Groot twisted his roots and dropped the blue creature to the floor. It lay there covering its face with its hands. Rocket and Groot strolled toward their cells, and Peter stepped over the moaning blue creature, looking out at all the inmates. He knew he was lucky to be under the protection of Groot. Nobody would mess with him now. "I'm with them," he said, just to confirm what everyone had seen.

Gamora was in more trouble. Many of the inmates still had a grudge against her because they knew she had worked with Ronan, and that night Peter woke up at the sound of a struggle. As he sat up in the middle of a bunch of other sleeping inmates, he saw a group dragging Gamora down the hall.

She might have been an assassin, but he couldn't just let her suffer whatever her enemies in the Kyln had planned. Peter got up and followed. Behind him, he heard Rocket mutter, "Quill. Where you going? Quill?"

A group of inmates pressed close around Gamora. One of them held a knife to her throat. "Gamora," he rasped, "consider this a death sentence for your crimes against the galaxy."

Peter didn't know what to do, and it turned out he didn't have to do anything right away because someone else had noticed the commotion. A shirtless, heavily muscled humanoid, his skin a swirl of red and green tattoos and ritual scars, stepped out of the shadows and said, "You dare!"

Gamora's would-be killers turned. When they saw who was speaking, looks of terror appeared on their faces and they backed away from her a little.

"You know who I am, yes?" the intruder asked.

"You're—you're Drax. The Destroyer," one of them said.

"You know why they call me this," Drax said as he approached the group.

"You've slain dozens of Ronan's minions." The inmate, who had been so bold with Gamora, looked like he wished he was anywhere else but facing Drax. Peter noticed Rocket next to him. They both watched the unfolding drama, wondering if they should intervene.

"Ronan murdered my wife, Ovette, and my daughter, Camaria. He slaughtered them where they stood and he laughed!" Drax said, his voice rising to a roar on the last word. "Her life is not yours to take. He killed my family. I shall kill one of his in return."

"Of course, Drax," the prisoner said. He bowed his head and held out his knife. "Here, I—"

Gamora saw everyone looking away from her, just for a

moment, and she seized the opportunity. She moved faster than Peter could follow. All he heard was bones cracking and inmates yelling, and when Gamora stopped again she had a knife in each hand. One was held at the throat of the prisoner who had been so eager to kill her. The other was laid against the top of Drax's collarbone, where an artery pulsed in his neck. He didn't look scared, but he also didn't test her by moving.

Peter started creeping into the room. "Quill!" Rocket hissed behind him. "What are you doing?"

Holding the knife at Drax's throat, Gamora said, "I'm no family to Ronan or Thanos." She took a step back and dropped the knives. "I'm your only hope of stopping them."

Drax paused, then lunged forward, picking up one of the knives. He gripped Gamora by the throat and forced her up against the wall, brandishing it in her face. "Woman, your words mean nothing to me!"

"Hey! Hey, hey, hey!" Peter called out, stepping into the room. He had to do something.

Behind him, he heard Rocket mutter, "Oh, crap."

"You know, if killing Ronan is truly your sole purpose," Peter said, "I don't think this is the best way to go about it." He advanced slowly, showing his hands so this Drax character wouldn't see him as a threat.

54

"Are you not the man this woman attempted to kill?" Drax asked.

"Well, I mean, she's hardly the first woman to try to do that to me," Peter said, trying to lighten the situation up a little. He showed Drax a scar on his side. "This is from a Rajak girl, tried to stab me with a fork. Right here a Kree girl tried to rip out my thorax," he added, pointing to another scar at the base of his neck. "She caught me with—"

Drax was just staring at him. "You don't care. But here's the point." Peter knew he'd gotten Drax's attention, and Gamora was still alive, so things were working out okay so far. "She betrayed Ronan. He's coming back for her. And when he does…"

Peter made a throat-cutting gesture. Drax looked puzzled. "Why would I put my finger on his throat?"

"What?" It took Peter a minute to figure out that Drax didn't understand the gesture. "Oh, no, it's a symbol." He repeated the gesture. "This is a symbol for you slicing his throat."

"I would not slice his throat," Drax said. "I would cut his head clean off."

"It's a general expression for you killing somebody." Peter turned to the other inmates. Didn't everyone know that gesture? "You've heard of this. You've seen this, right?"

"Yeah, yeah," the inmates said...but as soon as Drax looked at them, they all shook their heads. "No, no, no."

Peter gave up and got literal again. "What I'm saying is, you want to keep her alive. Don't do his work for him."

For a long moment Drax still held Gamora against the wall. Then he let go of her throat. She collapsed to the floor, gasping for breath. Drax walked out of the room. On his way he said to the ringleader of the inmates, "I like your knife. I'm keeping it."

A minute later, Peter was following Gamora back to her cell. "Listen," he said, "I couldn't care less whether you live or whether you die."

"Then why stop the big guy?" she asked.

"Simple. You know where to sell my Orb," Peter said.

She looked at him like he was an idiot. "How are we going to sell it when we and it are still here?"

Peter grinned. "My friend Rocket here has escaped twenty-two prisons."

"Oh, we're getting out," Rocket said. "And then we're headed straight to Yondu to retrieve your bounty."

This was not what Peter had in mind. "How much was your buyer willing to pay you for my Orb?"

She paused. "Four billion units."

"What?" Peter and Rocket said simultaneously.

"That Orb is my opportunity to get away from Thanos and Ronan," Gamora said. "If you free us, I'll lead you to the buyer directly and I'll split the profit between the three of us."

Four billion units. Even split three ways, that was enough that none of them would ever have to work again. They'd be lying awake at night thinking of ways to spend their money.

"I am Groot," said Groot from the other side of the fence separating the hall from his cell.

"Four of us," Rocket said. "Asleep for the danger, awake for the money, as per usual."

Groot growled, but the deal was struck. Now it was time to plan the escape.

CHAPTER 5

On the *Dark Aster*, Ronan received unwelcome news from an emissary of Thanos, who was present via an animated projection on the wall of the ship's throne room. "You have been betrayed, Ronan," the emissary said.

"We know only that she has been captured," Ronan said correctly. "Gamora may yet recover the Orb."

"No!" the emissary snapped. "Our sources within the Kyln say Gamora has her own plans for the Orb. Look, your partnership with Thanos is at risk. Thanos requires your presence. Now!"

The emissary's masked face disappeared from the wall.

Ronan turned to look at Nebula. She returned his look and said nothing...but she didn't have to. Ronan could tell what she was thinking. She was enjoying his discomfort, and she believed he should have sent her instead of Gamora. Perhaps she was correct, but Ronan would not admit that...to her or anyone else.

Ronan traveled immediately to the rocky domain known as Sanctuary. The emissary conducted him to an open rocky cliff, where the throne of Thanos floated with its back to Ronan. "With all due respect, Thanos, your daughter made this mess, and yet you summon me," he began.

"I would lower my voice, Accuser," the emissary warned.

Ronan ignored him. "First, she lost a battle with some primitive."

"Thanos put Gamora under your charge," the emissary interrupted.

Ronan was very close to losing his temper at the emissary's scorn and impudence, but he kept his focus on Thanos. "Then she was apprehended by the Nova Corps," he went on.

"You are the one here with nothing to show for it!" the emissary spat.

Still Ronan continued. "Your sources say that she meant to betray us the whole time!"

"Lower your tone!" the emissary commanded. Before he could go on, Ronan snapped. A bolt of force from the Cosmi-Rod cracked the emissary's head around violently. He dropped without another sound.

All the while, Nebula sat off to the side and watched. She was using a small laser to make adjustments to some of the cybernetic components in her left arm.

"I only ask that you take this matter seriously," Ronan finished.

Thanos's throne, a levitating chair made of stone and technology so ancient yet advanced that Ronan did not know how it worked, turned slowly around. "The only matter I do not take seriously, boy, is you," Thanos said. Facing Ronan, he leaned forward, eyes glittering under his helmet and anger clear on his ravaged purple face. "Your politics bore me. Your demeanor is that of a pouty child. And apparently you alienated my favorite daughter, Gamora."

Out of the corner of his eye, Ronan saw Nebula react to this. Her father's remark stung her. He filed that away. Her resentment might one day be useful to him.

"I shall honor our agreement, Kree...if you bring me the Orb," Thanos said. "But return to me again empty-handed, and I will bathe the starways in your blood."

Nebula stood. "Thanks, Dad. Sounds fair." She started walking back toward Ronan's ship. "This is one fight you won't win," she said to him as she passed. "Let's head to the Kyln."

The next morning, over steel trays of some of the most disgusting "food" Peter had ever smelled, Rocket explained what he needed for his escape plan.

"If we're gonna get out of here, we're gonna need to get into the watchtower," the furry little alien said, jerking his head back at the central guard post. "And to do that, I'm gonna need a few things. The guards wear security bands to control their ins and outs. I need one." Peter remembered Rocket watching the guard on their way into the Kyln. He'd already been planning this escape, Peter realized.

"Leave it to me," Gamora said.

"That dude there," Rocket said, pointing to a prisoner who limped along using a robotic leg replacement. "I need his prosthetic leg."

"His leg?" Peter repeated. What good would that do them?

"Yeah. God knows I don't need the rest of him. Look at him, he's useless," Rocket said.

"All right," Peter said uncertainly.

"And finally, on the wall back there is a black panel. Blinky yellow light. You see it?"

Peter glanced over and saw the panel, maybe twenty feet above the floor on the guard tower wall. "Yeah."

"There's a quarnyx battery behind it. Purplish box, green wires. To get into that watchtower, I definitely need that."

"How are we supposed to do that?" Gamora asked.

"Well, supposedly these bald bodies find you attractive," Rocket said. "So maybe you can..."

"You must be joking," she said.

"No, I really heard they find you attractive," Rocket said, not missing a beat.

"Look, it's twenty feet up in the air, and it's in the middle of the most heavily guarded part of the prison," Peter said. "It's impossible to get up there without being seen."

"I got one plan, and that plan requires a quarnyx battery, so figure it out!" Rocket snarled. He looked from Peter to Gamora. "Now, can I get back to it? Thanks. Once the battery is removed, everything is going to slam into emergency mode. Once we have it, we gotta move quickly, so you definitely need to get that last."

As Rocket finished his sentence, the entire station dimmed. A split-second after, red emergency lighting glowed throughout the prison area, an alarm went off, and armed guards started to swarm into the yard.

Rocket looked up and saw Groot extending the quarnyx battery toward him, clearly very pleased with himself. On the wall, sparks shot from the hole recently covered by the black panel.

"Or we could just get it first and improvise," Rocket said with a sigh.

Gamora stood. "I'll get the armband."

"Leg," Peter said as he ran off through the crowd.

Alarms kept blaring and the prisoners, realizing what was happening, quickly worked themselves up into a full-blown riot.

Drones swooped into the common area and circled Groot. "Prisoner, drop the device immediately and retreat to your cell, or we will open fire," a guard ordered over the speakers. Groot turned, trying to keep track of all the drones. Spikes grew out of his shoulders and back. "I am Groot!!!" he roared, still holding the battery.

"Fire!" the guard said. The drones unleashed a hail of automatic slugs, peppering Groot but only making him angry. He swiped at one of the drones, slapping it across the common area to crash under a walkway. It exploded, and prisoners scattered away. Groot hit another of the drones, which tumbled up and shattered on an upper cell level.

"All prisoners, return to your sleeping areas," the guard ordered, but if anyone was paying attention, Peter didn't see it. He ran, dodging ricocheting slugs from the drones, and went looking for the inmate with the prosthetic leg.

Rocket was also dodging the drones' fire, but he was on his way toward Groot. Climbing up onto Groot's shoulder, he shouted over the commotion. "You idiot! How am I supposed to fight these things without my stuff?"

A drone hovered right in front of Groot and he sprouted a shield of brambles and branches from his arm. The drone's fire chewed splinters and bits of twig from the shield, but he didn't go down. When the drone paused to reload, Groot smashed it away with the shield. That left his back exposed to a squad of guards who were responding from the watchtower.

"The animal's in control!" one of them shouted. "Fire on my command."

Drax watched as they all aimed their weapons at Rocket. Then, just before they fired, he leapt into action. It was one against six—and the guards never had a chance. Laughing maniacally the whole time, Drax flung one of them away to collide with a second, dropped a third with a pulverizing punch, jerked the gun from a fourth and threw it to crack into the fifth, and only then did the fourth guard manage to hit him. Drax stared at the guard like he couldn't believe what had just happened. Then he head-butted him, knocking the guard sprawling. The last guard turned to shoot, but Drax lifted him up and smashed him to the floor.

He stood with the last guard's weapon in his hand. "Creepy little beast!" he called.

Rocket looked up. Drax threw the weapon. Rocket's eyes lit up as he caught it. "Oh, yeah," he said.

He cocked it and squeezed the trigger, blasting away at the drones and the guards and everything else that looked like a threat. Groot turned, giving Rocket a full three-hundred-and-sixty-degree field of fire. Whatever else happened, the guards were going to remember Rocket.

Meanwhile, Peter had found the inmate he was looking for. "You need my what?" he asked.

Peter made him an offer he couldn't refuse.

On another level, and across the common area, Gamora fought her way through a detachment of guards. She wasn't looking for a fight, but she couldn't very well get one of the control armbands while people were shooting at her. She vaulted over a railing and kicked a guard to the ground, then ducked a baton swing from another before grabbing his arm to keep him in one place while she knocked him out with an elbow. Two more guards were coming, and one had a riot shield. She charged straight at them, hitting the shield so it bounced away off the railing, and slammed the guard to the ground. Then she spun and locked one leg around the last guard as he tried to stun her with his baton. He had one of the armbands. "I'll need this," she said.

"Good luck," he sneered. "It's internally wired."

"I'll figure something out," she said.

Peter was running down the corridor with the prisoner's leg, back out to where the others were, when he was spotted by a guard. "Drop the leg!" the guard shouted, his gun leveled at Peter. "Drop the leg and move back to your cell!"

Peter lowered the leg as if he was going to drop it—then swung it hard, knocking the guard's gun barrel to the side. With his return swing, he targeted the guard's head. The guard went down and Peter picked up his gun just in time to shoot down a drone that would have blown him away. Keeping both the gun and the leg, he ran back down to meet Rocket and Groot.

Rocket ran out of ammo just as Gamora called to him from a nearby catwalk. He turned and caught the armband she threw toward him. "Move to the watchtower!" he said, and Groot lumbered in that direction. Rocket hummed a tune as he used the quarnyx battery and the armband to put together a little something special.

When Groot got to the watchtower, he sprouted himself taller, his arms reaching up to the level where Gamora was running around to meet them. Peter was climbing up with the leg from below. He had a scare when a drone hummed up and aimed its weapon at him, but out of nowhere the crazy tattooed guy. Drax leaped up and caught the drone in his bare hands!

The drone blasted away at Drax, but its weapons couldn't hurt him. He flexed his muscles and tore it in two, then threw the pieces away. Peter nodded his thanks and kept climbing. Drax was right behind him.

"We need all available guards in full combat gear," the officer in the watchtower's command center was saying when his door alarm went off. He turned to see Rocket, Groot, Peter, Gamora, and Drax standing in the doorway. After a moment, he raised his hands.

When they had control of the room, Gamora pointed at Drax. "Why is this one here?" she asked, clearly not happy about it.

"We promised him he could stay by your side until he kills your boss," Peter explained. "I always keep my promises when they're to muscle-bound wack jobs who will kill me if I don't. Here you go," he added to Rocket, holding out the prosthetic leg.

"Oh, I was just kidding about the leg," Rocket said with a shrug. "I just need these two things."

"What?" Peter shouted.

"I thought it'd be funny! Was it funny?" Rocket was cracking himself up. "What did he look like hopping around?"

"I had to transfer him thirty thousand units," Peter complained.

"How are we going to leave?" Drax asked, cutting through Rocket's chuckles.

"Well, he's got a plan," Peter said. "Right? Or is that another thing you made up?"

"I have a plan," Rocket said as he dug around in the control center's wiring.

"Cease your yammering and relieve us from this irksome confinement," Drax said.

Peter nodded. A drone was firing at them from outside, but its slugs couldn't penetrate the armored windows and walls. "Yeah, I'll have to agree with the walking thesaurus on that one," he said.

"Do not ever call me a thesaurus," Drax said, his voice low and deadly.

Surprised, Peter said, "It's just a metaphor, dude."

"His people are completely literal," Rocket said, still working. "Metaphors are gonna go over his head."

"Nothing goes over my head," Drax said, inadvertently proving Rocket's point. "My reflexes are too fast. I would catch it."

"I'm going to die surrounded by the biggest idiots in the galaxy," Gamora lamented.

Peter looked out the window, checking out the action in the yard. He didn't like what he saw. "Those are some big guns," he said, pointing down to four arriving Nova Guards with giant shoulder-mounted rocket launchers. The guards aimed the launchers up at the tower where they were standing.

KA-BOOOOM! The whole watchtower shook as one of the Nova Guard's rockets slammed into the reinforced window. It left a big crack, but the window held.

"Rodent, we are ready for your plan," Gamora said.

Rocket was working frantically. "Hold on!"

A second rocket cracked the window more. It was only a matter of time if Rocket's plan didn't work.

"I recognize this animal," Drax suddenly said. "We'd roast them over a flame pit as children. Their flesh was quite delicious."

"Not helping!" Rocket shouted at Drax.

A third rocket spiderwebbed the window. Small pieces fell out of it. The next one would punch through and explode inside the watchtower. "All fire on my command!" the guard officer shouted from below. "Three...two...!"

Rocket held up two connectors and jammed them together.

Peter was expecting something spectacular, but Rocket's

plan was more subtle and effective. The only sound was a droopy mechanical groan, and outside the tower, everything changed. Guards, prisoners, furniture, even bits of destroyed drones, floated gently off the ground. Everyone flailed to keep his or her balance.

"He turned off the artificial gravity...everywhere but in here," Gamora observed. She smiled in appreciation of Rocket's maneuver.

But Rocket wasn't done. He pushed a lever on the command console and explosive bolts below the command center fired. The center floated free from the top of the tower. Then Rocket slaved all of the remaining drones. They flew toward the floating command center module and gripped on to its base. Using one of the controls like a joystick, Rocket guided the hover-bots as they pushed the module out of the cellblock.

Watching the guards and prisoners flail in zero-G, Rocket smiled. "I told you I had a plan."

He slammed the module through a door and bounced it down a long service corridor, scattering Kyln guards along the way and scraping off some of the drones in showers of sparks. When the module came to rest and Rocket had shut a blast door behind them, Peter nodded. "That was a pretty good plan."

They got out of the module and recovered their stuff from the impound lockers. "There it is! Get my ship," Peter said to Rocket. "It's the *Milano*, the orange-and-blue one over in the corner."

"They crumpled my pants up into a ball!" Rocket complained. "That's rude. They folded yours."

Peter was digging through his things with Gamora looking over his shoulder. "The Orb's there. Let's go," she said when he found it in his backpack.

"Wait, wait, wait," Peter said, digging around in the locker. "That bastard didn't put it back." Awesome Mix Tape Vol. 1 wasn't there!

Peter handed his backpack to Gamora. "Here. Get them to the ship. I'll be right back."

"How are you going to possibly—?"

Peter turned to run back toward the station. "Just keep the *Milano* close by. Go."

He ran back into the interior of the Kyln. On the way, he put on his mask again. This was a job for Star-Lord.

CHAPTER 6

eter shot his way through the Kyln guards with his blasters, leaving them in twitching heaps. He stepped over their bodies and headed for the last place he'd seen his tape player.

Gamora led Rocket, Groot, and Drax aboard the *Milano*. Once in the cockpit, Rocket started booting up the ship's controls.

"How's he gonna get to us?" Rocket asked Gamora, annoyed.

"He declined to share that information with me," Gamora stated.

"Well, forget this!" shouted Rocket. "I ain't waiting around for some humie with a death wish. You got the Orb, right?"

"Yes," said Gamora, opening Peter's backpack. But when she looked in, all she saw was a bunch of junk. With a frustrated sigh, she looked over at Rocket, who looked ready to kill someone.

Peter had made sure they wouldn't leave without him.

Deep inside the station, Peter casually tossed the Orb in the air as he neared the main office. Inside, the guard who had stolen his headphones was still sitting at his desk, bopping his head to Peter's favorite songs. This guy didn't even seem to know there was a riot going on! He was apparently missing the whole thing while grooving to Awesome Mix Tape Vol. 1.

Peter lifted the Orb in the air and tapped the guard on the shoulder to get his attention. When the guard looked up, Peter knocked him out cold with the Orb.

Back on the *Milano*, tensions were running high.

"If we don't leave now, we will be blown to bits," Rocket argued, jumping into the pilot seat.

"No!" Gamora said. "We're not leaving without the Orb."

Their argument might have escalated, but right then

Drax saw something out the cockpit window. "Behold," he said, and they all turned to see Peter Quill—Star-Lord—flying around the outside of the Kyln toward the *Milano*.

They met him as he entered the ship through a secondary airlock. "This one shows spirit!" Drax said. "He will make a keen ally in the battle against Ronan. Companion, what were you retrieving?"

Peter pulled the tape player out of his jacket, ejected the tape, and handed the player to Drax. He looked it over and his expression changed.

"You are an imbecile," he said darkly.

After they'd made their escape, there was nothing to do but kill time until they got to the place where Gamora had said the exchange could take place. Everyone did their own thing and for Rocket that meant taking things apart and putting them back together so they were more deadly. Peter ran across him sitting in a pile of machinery and components in the back of the ship. "Whoa, whoa! Hey, what are you doing? You can't take apart my ship without asking me!" He bent down to pick up something Rocket had apparently made. "What is this?"

"Don't touch that," Rocket said. "It's a bomb."

"A bomb?"

"Yup."

"And you leave it lying around?"

"I was gonna put it in a box," Rocket said.

"What's a box gonna do?" Peter shouted.

Ignoring him, Rocket picked up a brightly colored object and looked at it. "What's this one?"

It was the present Peter's mother had given him right before she died. He'd never opened it. "Whoa, leave it alone!" Peter grabbed it.

"Why, what is it?"

"Shut up!"

"Hey." Rocket shrugged, and got back to work.

Despite his irritation, Peter was interested in what Rocket was doing. "What is that?" he asked, pointing.

"That's for if things get really hard-core," Rocket said. "Or if you want to blow up moons."

"No one's blowing up moons," Gamora said.

"You just want to suck the joy out of everything," Rocket grumbled.

Still holding on to the present, Peter went over to a star map. "So, listen, I'm gonna need your buyer's coordinates," he said to Gamora.

"We're heading in the right direction. For now." She picked up the Orb and looked it over.

"If we're going to work together, you might want to try trusting me a little bit."

"And how much do you trust me?" she countered.

He took the Orb from her. "I'd trust you a lot more if you told me what this was. Because I'm guessing it's some kind of weapon."

"I don't know what it is," she said.

Drax picked up the Orb. "If it's a weapon we should use it against Ronan."

"Put it down, you fool. You'll destroy us all," Gamora snapped.

"Or just you, murderess!"

"I let you live once, princess," she said, stepping up to him.

Infuriated, Drax shouted, "I am not a princess!"

"Hey!" They both looked at Peter. "Nobody is killing anybody on my ship! We're stuck together until we get the money."

Drax snorted. "I have no interest in money." He tossed the Orb back to Peter.

"Great," Peter said. "That means more money for the three of us."

Groot grunted.

"For the four of us," Peter corrected himself. "Partners."

"We have an agreement, but I would never be partners with the likes of you," Gamora said. "I'll tell the buyer we're on our way. And, Quill, your ship is filthy." She left, going up the stairs to the crew quarters.

"Oh, she has no idea," Peter chuckled.

CHAPTER 7

Soon after the *Milano*'s escape, Ronan's ship, the *Dark Aster*, attacked the Kyln. Already damaged from the riot and short on staff, the station didn't have adequate defenses to fight against Ronan's assault. His forces tore through the walls like they were made out of paper and had both the inmates and the guards under control before a distress call could even be sent out.

As Ronan strode through the station, he was flooded with thoughts. Nebula broke off her interrogation of a prisoner and got his attention. "Ronan. The Nova Corps have sent a fleet to defend the prison. It should be here shortly."

"Well, then. Send the Necrocraft to every corner of the quadrant," commanded Ronan, his anger rising. "Find the Orb. Any means, any price."

Nebula bowed again, acknowledging Ronan's will. "And...this place?" she asked.

"The Nova can't learn what we're after," said Ronan. "Cleanse it."

Yondu had finally made his way from Morag to the Broker's shop on Xandar. He'd had to dodge a few Nova Corps patrols along the way, which had slowed him down. Now he was intent on finding out what the Broker knew about where Quill might have gone with the Orb.

"You got any other cute little buggers like this one?" he asked, tapping the glass cover of a display case containing small ornaments. "I like to stick 'em all in a row on my control console."

"I can't tell if you're joking or not," the Broker said from behind his desk.

"He's being fully serious," confirmed the Ravager standing guard by the door.

The Broker came around his desk and fished the key to the case out of his coat pocket. "In that case, I can show you—"

Yondu cut him off. "But first you gonna tell me what this Orb is, and why everybody cares so much about it. And then you gonna tell me who out there might want to buy it."

"Sir," the Broker said. "The high-end community is..."

"Blah blah bobuley blah," Yondu said.

The Broker tried again. "...is a very tight-knit..."

Yondu interrupted him with gibberish again.

"I cannot possibly betray the confidence of my buyers," the Broker insisted.

Yondu opened his coat, uncovering the steel arrow at his belt. Its tip glowed, and at a whistle from Yondu it shot out and hovered with its point less than an inch from the Broker's forehead. The Broker stumbled backward against his desk.

Yondu chuckled. The metal fin on the top of his skull glowed the same bright red as the tip of the arrow. "Now, who again is this buyer of yours?" he asked.

Peter was practicing his quick draws in the *Milano*'s lounge when he heard Rocket call down from the cockpit. "Heads up! We're inbound!"

He went upstairs and looked out the cockpit window to see...well, a brand-new thing, unlike any other sight he'd ever encountered in his travels through the galaxy. It was a planetoid-size space station, in the shape of a giant skull. Its eyes were metallic orbs, and where its teeth would have been, Peter could see structures large enough for thousands of people to inhabit.

"Whoa," he said.

Drax frowned in puzzlement. "What is it?"

"It's called Knowhere," Gamora said. "The severed head of an ancient celestial being," Gamora reported matter-of-factly, as if this were the most normal information in the galaxy. "Be wary going in, rodent. There are no regulations whatsoever here."

Peter steered the ship through one of the giant skull's eye sockets. When the *Milano* had passed into what would have been the skull's braincase, they saw an entire city built into the bone walls. Miners flying single-person space pods were drilling into spots around the skull, extracting what looked like a yellow viscous fluid. Robots carrying other material flew between different parts of the city.

"Hundreds of years ago, the Tivan Group sent workers in to mine the organic matter within the skull," explained Gamora after they had docked. "Bone, brain tissue, spinal fluid. All rare resources, highly valued in black markets across the galaxy. It's dangerous, illegal work suitable only for outlaws."

"Well, I come from a planet of outlaws," Peter boasted as they navigated the crowd. Knowhere seemed like a typical mining town, if it weren't for the surreal fact that it was built inside a giant dead alien's head. "Billy the Kid, Bonnie and Clyde..."

"It sounds like a place that I would like to visit," said Drax.

Peter nodded. "Yeah, you should."

A group of child beggars surrounded them, asking for spare units. "Watch your wallets," Peter said. But Groot—who had no wallet to worry about—leaned down toward one of the group, a girl about ten years old. He opened his palm, and a tiny blue flower grew from it. Groot picked the bloom and handed it to the girl. She accepted it, an expression of wonder on her face.

"Get out of here," Peter said to the rest of them, and they moved on toward a tavern. A sign at the entrance said it was the Boot of Jemiah.

"Your buyer's in there?" Rocket asked Gamora.

"We are to wait here for his representative," she said. As they approached the door, a bouncer was throwing a man out into the street. It looked to be a pretty rough bar, even by the standards of a deep-space mining complex.

"This is no respectable establishment," Drax said. "What do you expect us to do while we wait?"

It didn't take long to answer Drax's question. Within minutes, Rocket had shown Groot and Drax the small track where Orloni races were held. The Orloni, small, ratlike rodents, raced down a track to escape a hungry frog-beast called a F'Saki. Rocket loved Orloni races, and the competition naturally appealed to Drax. Soon he was cheering and roaring as loudly as the rest of the patrons crowded around the table.

"My Orloni has won, as I win at all things!" Drax crowed. "Now let's put more of this liquid into our bodies."

"That's the first thing you've said that wasn't crazy!" Rocket laughed.

Meanwhile, on the other side of the room, Peter joined

Gamora at a railing looking out of the exterior of the skull to the galaxy. "Man, you wouldn't believe what they charge for fuel out here," Peter said. "I might actually lose money on this job."

"My connection is making us wait," Gamora complained.

"It's just a negotiation tactic," explained Peter. "Trust me, this is my specialty. Where yours is more: 'Stab, stab. Those are my terms.'"

Gamora smiled at him, and Peter was surprised to find that her smile made him happy. "My father didn't stress diplomacy."

"Thanos?" asked Peter.

Just as quickly as it had come, her smile vanished. "Thanos is not my father. When Thanos took my home world, he killed my parents in front of me. He turned me into a weapon. When he said he was going to destroy an entire planet for Ronan, I couldn't stand by and..." She trailed off. Then she changed the subject, pointing to the tape player stuck into Peter's belt.

"Why would you risk your life for this?" Gamora asked. She pulled it out and pressed play. One of the softer songs on Awesome Mix Tape Vol. 1 filled the air between them.

"My mother gave it to me," he explained. "My mom

liked sharing with me all the pop songs she loved growing up. I happened to have it on me when I was...the day that she...you know. When I left Earth."

"What do you do with it?" Gamora asked.

"Do? Nothing. You listen to it. Or you can dance."

"I am a warrior and an assassin," stated Gamora flatly. "I do not dance."

"Really," Peter said. "Well, on my planet there's a legend about people like you. In it, a great hero named Kevin teaches an entire city that dancing, well...it's the greatest thing there is."

Peter slipped the headphones over Gamora's ears and hit play. She cocked her head, listening to a slow jam.

"The melody is pleasant!" she shouted, not used to talking with headphones on. Peter started to move with the song. He took Gamora's hand and felt her start to move with him. They started dancing. Gamora was clearly amazed at what she was allowing herself to do. Their faces drifted closer, almost to kissing distance—

Then all of a sudden Peter found himself spun around and slammed against the rail with one of Gamora's many knives at his throat. "Whoa!" he shouted.

"I know who you are, Peter Quill!" she said. "And I am not some starry-eyed waif about to succumb to your—"

"That is not what's happening," he protested.

She let him go and at that moment both of them heard an eruption in the crowd back by the Orloni table. They turned to see Groot and Drax roll across the table and onto the floor, fighting with everything they had.

"Oh, no," Peter said. The fight was bad enough, but he was sure he and Gamora had been having a moment. He sighed and ran to break it up.

CHAPTER 8

Peter and Gamora sprinted for the Orloni table, arriving just as Drax tore himself free of Groot's roots—and just as Rocket was about to escalate the situation with his favorite gun. "Whoa! Whoa! Whoa! What're you doing?" yelled Peter, waving his arms and getting in front of Rocket.

"This vermin speaks of affairs he knows nothing about!" shouted Drax, as Gamora held him back.

"That is true!" confirmed Rocket.

"He has no respect!" Drax shouted even louder.

"Keep calling me 'vermin,' tough guy," Rocket growled. "You just wanna laugh at me like everyone else!"

"Rocket," Peter said, stepping closer to him. "No one's laughing at you."

Rocket's voice was raw and he seemed on the verge of tears. "He thinks I'm some stupid thing! He does! Well, I didn't ask to get made! I didn't ask to be torn apart and put back together, over and over until I'm..." He took a deep breath, almost a sob. "Some little monster!"

Peter kept trying to calm him down. "Rocket, no one's calling you a monster."

But Rocket pushed Peter away. "He called me 'vermin'! She called me 'rodent'! Let's see if you can laugh after five or six shots to your face!"

He raised his weapon again and, as it powered up, Peter jumped right in front of the muzzle again. "No, no, no, no!" he shouted. "Four billion units, man! Come on, suck it up for one more lousy night and you're rich!"

That got Rocket's attention. He took a deep breath and looked around at all of them. Then he dropped his gaze and powered down his weapon. "Fine. But I can't promise when this is all over I'm not going to kill every last one of you jerks."

Man, Peter thought. *You can't help but feel bad for the little guy, but, even so, why is everyone always waving guns around?* "See, that's exactly why none of you have any

89

friends," Peter said. "Five seconds after you meet somebody, you're already trying to kill them."

While Rocket had calmed down somewhat, Drax was still visibly angry. "We have traveled halfway across the quadrant and all I have done is quarrel with wildlife," complained Drax as he left. "And Ronan is no closer to being dead!"

And with that, Drax shoved through the crowd toward the exit, leaving Peter to call after him.

"Let him go. We don't need him," said Gamora to Peter.

At that moment, a hidden panel in one of the club's walls opened up, revealing a small humanoid female in a dress that reminded Peter of a fairy tale. She stepped forward, addressing Gamora. "Milady Gamora. I am here to fetch you for my master."

Gamora, Peter, Groot, and Rocket looked at one another. Finally, it was go time. They followed Carina through a secret passage into a dark tunnel. After some distance, the tunnel opened up into a large room lined with glass cages. The cages were filled with animals, plants, and other... life-forms? Peter could only guess. It occurred to him that not too long ago, he'd been thinking of all the amazing things he'd seen in his travels through space. Now he'd seen at least as many amazing things just in the past few days, since he first laid eyes on the Orb. And high up on the weird-but-amazing list was this combination zoo-museum, which went on for as far as the eye could see. It seemed to stretch on forever, like it had once been a dream belonging to the dead giant alien whose head they were all roaming around in.

"Oookay," Rocket said. "This isn't creepy at all."

Carina led the group onward to an examination bay while explaining, "We house the galaxy's largest collection of fauna, relics, and species of all manner." As they reached the top of the stairs, strange growls and chirps reached them from the thousands of cells and tanks holding the Collector's specimens.

Ahead of them, engrossed in the study of one of those specimens, was a human male—or at least what looked like one from behind. Carina introduced him: "I present to you Taneleer Tivan: the Collector."

Tivan, Peter thought. The name of the company that had started mining the alien head. Apparently it was a family business.

The Collector turned around, giving them a moment to absorb his appearance. His hair was white and exploded out from his head in a wave. He wore goggles that appeared to have several different devices built into the lenses. Over his shoulder lay a fur stole of some kind, contrasting oddly with the subdued black of the rest of his clothing. He took off the goggles and stepped forward to greet Gamora, taking her hand and bowing his head to kiss it.

"My dear Gamora," he said, his voice a slow purr. "How wonderful to meet in the flesh."

"Let's bypass the formalities, Tivan," Gamora said, although she didn't take her hand back. "We have what we discussed."

Over her shoulder, the Collector spied Groot. A strange expression, almost hunger, appeared on his face. "What is that thing there?"

"I am Groot."

The Collector moved past Gamora, ignoring the rest of them. "I never thought I'd meet a Groot," he said, looking Groot up and down. "Sir. You must allow me to pay you now so that I may own your carcass...at the moment of your death, of course."

Groot shrugged. "I am Groot."

"Why? So he can turn you into a chair?" Rocket asked.

The Collector glanced down at Rocket, then back up to Groot. "That's your pet?"

"His what?!?" shouted Rocket. He started to unshoulder his rifle.

Seeing where this was likely to go, Gamora interrupted. "Tivan, we've been halfway around the galaxy retrieving this Orb."

"Very well, then, let us see what you've bought," said the Collector. Peter took the Orb out of his bag and promptly dropped it on the floor. He scooped it up, covering his embarrassment, and held it out to the Collector.

After a moment spent carefully looking it over, the Collector smiled. "Oh, my new friends," intoned the Collector. "Before creation itself, there were six singularities." He placed the Orb in a device composed of two claw arms that reached out and began to twist it apart into two halves. A purple hologram spawned in the air over the work table, the same color as the glow that became visible from inside the Orb as the Collector's machine unlocked it. A series of clicks and whirs accompanied his voice. "Then the universe exploded into existence and the remnants of these systems were forged into six ingots."

The hologram divided into spheres, each containing

a different color of what looked like crystals. "Infinity Stones," the Collector went on. "These Stones, it seems, can only be brandished by beings of extraordinary strength. Observe."

One of the spherical holograms changed—the purple one. Now it displayed a huge mechanical construct, wielding a staff whose head glowed the same purple as the inside of the Orb. Thousands of humanoids fled the construct. It struck its staff against the ground, and a wave of destruction overwhelmed the fleeing people...leaving nothing behind but ash and speckles of glowing purple.

"These carriers can use the Stones to mow down entire civilizations like wheat in a field," the Collector said as the hologram view pulled back to reveal the entire planet overrun by the purple energy. "Once, for a moment, a group was able to share the energy amongst themselves, but even they were quickly destroyed by it."

His machine finished its work and pulled the two halves of the Orb apart. Hanging in the air over the table between them was a glowing purple Stone. The Collector looked down at it and a tremor went through his body. "Beautiful," he crooned. "Beyond compare."

"Blah, blah, blah," Rocket cut in. "We're all very fascinated, whitey. But we'd like to get paid."

"How would you like to get paid?"

"What do you think, fancy man? Units!"

"Very well, then." The Collector opened a drawer and reached in. Then he noticed Carina, stepping closer to the glowing Infinity Stone on the nearby table. "Carina," he warned. "Stand back."

She had been watching and waiting for a moment such as this. For years she'd suffered under the cruel hand of the Collector, who badly mistreated her and her fellow servants. One of her predecessors had even been added to his collection, near where Carina slept—as a reminder, she knew, and a warning. She had heard the Collector talking about this Orb and the power that it held, and she was convinced that if she could hold such power in her hand, she would be able to free herself from her cruel master.

But, unfortunately for Carina, she didn't understand the nature of that power.

"I will no longer be your slave!" Carina shouted. She lunged for the Stone and grasped it in her hand.

"No!" shouted the Collector ... but it was too late.

The moment Carina touched the Stone, her whole body convulsed. Her eyes bulged and turned black; her face distorted with energy. A fierce purple glow—exactly the same as what they had just seen on the Collector's hologram—began to crackle out from under her skin. She screamed, but it was already too late. The energy from the Infinity Stone churned through every molecule of her body, spilling out in a series of small explosions. Groot picked up Rocket and ran. Gamora dragged Peter down behind a nearby table, hoping that would be enough protection. All of them could see what was coming.

The final explosion blasted out most of the windows in the Collector's museum. Rocket and Groot tumbled out into the street near the Boot, just ahead of the blast wave. Peter and Gamora hunkered down and felt it pass over them, rocking the table. Under the sound of the explosion they heard shattering glass and the crash of collapsing cases. Most of the Collector's collection vanished in a moment.

The Collector himself lay stunned in the wreckage, Peter noted as he and Gamora got up and looked for the Orb. It was still where the Collector had placed it. Gamora ran to the worktable and slammed the two halves of the Orb shut again. Then she and Peter headed for the exit, not bothering to check on the Collector. Gamora knew he could take care of himself—and she also knew that after what had just happened, there was no way they were going to get paid.

"How could I think Tivan could contain whatever was within the Orb?" shouted Gamora as they came back out into the street. As soon as they walked out of the passage, Rocket spied the Orb in her hand and started freaking out. "What do you still have it for?" he asked incredulously.

"What are we going to do?" Peter responded. "Leave it in there?"

"I can't believe you had that in your purse!"

"It's not a purse, it's a knapsack," Peter argued.

"We have to bring this to the Nova Corps. There's a chance they can contain it," Gamora said.

Rocket's eyes went wide. "Are you kidding me? We're wanted by the Nova Corps. Just give it to Ronan!"

Peter couldn't believe what he was hearing. "So he can destroy the galaxy?"

"What are you, some saint all of a sudden?" Rocket screeched. "What has the galaxy ever done for you? Why would you want to save it?"

"Because I'm one of the idiots who lives in it!"

"Peter, listen to me," Gamora interrupted. "We cannot allow the Orb to fall into Ronan's hands. We have to go back to your ship and deliver it to Nova!"

"Right, okay, I think you're right," Peter said. Gamora

tried to take the Orb from him, but he held on to it to keep her attention on him. "Or we bring it to someone who's not going to arrest us, who's really nice, for a whole lot of money."

She yanked it away.

"I think it's a really good balance between both your points of view," he suggested, looking from her to Rocket.

Gamora glared at him. "You're despicable. Dishonorable. Faithless!" She turned her back on him and strode away—and then she stopped, staring at something up in sky. Which, in Knowhere, was the inside of a giant skull, but it still felt like sky.

What she saw, and what Peter saw when he followed her gaze, was Drax, his back to them and his arms outstretched with a blade in each hand. He laughed like a maniac and looked up at a fleet of Necrocraft, the light striking ships from the fleet of Ronan the Accuser.

"At last, I shall meet my foe and destroy him!" said Drax, watching the ships come in for a landing.

"You called Ronan!?" Peter couldn't believe it. Even Drax wasn't that crazy, was he?

"Quill!" shouted a voice from across the street. Peter looked up to see Yondu! He and the other Ravagers were headed right for Peter. "Don't you move, boy," Yondu growled. Oh, man, didn't that just figure. Ronan showed up, and there was Yondu right at the same time, and both of them gunning for Peter and his friends. When it rained, it poured.

CHAPTER 9

Stand behind me!" Drax shouted to his companions, a smile on his face. "You may write of this tale in your storybooks, so that future generations shall delight in its telling!"

"I am Groot?" asked Groot.

"Yes, he is insane," said Rocket, answering Groot's question.

"Sanity is the refuge of cowards!" Drax declared.

Gamora moved quickly. Grabbing Peter, she ran off with Rocket and Groot on her tail. The Ravagers, seeing the Orb still in Gamora's hand, gave chase. They ran past

Drax, who held his ground in the street, watching, pleased, as all the Necrocraft now opened their doors.

Gamora ran up a ramp onto a loading station where a miner was anchoring his pod to a dock. Gamora grabbed the miner. "Try to curl up as you land," she advised him. He looked confused until she physically threw him off the ramp and down to the street below.

The mining pods were the kind Peter had seen from the *Milano* when they'd first docked at Knowhere. Small, single-person capsules with jets, they had robotic arms mounted to the front that were primarily used for operating mining equipment that drilled into the bone walls of the station.

Gamora quickly loaded herself into one pod, Peter into another, and Rocket into a third. "I told you, you can't fit," shouted Rocket to Groot as his pod took off. "Now wait here. I'll be back." Groot watched sadly as his friends zipped away.

By the time Yondu and the Ravagers reached the pod ramp, everyone was gone but Groot.

"Ronan the Accuser!" Drax shouted as he saw his sworn enemy exit one of the Necrocraft. The day of vengeance Drax had dreamed of was finally here! The battle, he was sure, would be glorious.

Ronan strode right up to Drax. "You are the one who transmitted the message?"

"You killed my wife. You killed my daughter!" shouted Drax, ignoring the question.

He might have gone on, but the conversation was interrupted when Nebula saw the mining pods streak overhead and shouted, "It is Gamora. She is escaping with the Orb!"

Without another thought for Drax, Ronan turned. "Nebula, retrieve the Orb." She disappeared into her Necrocraft and followed Gamora. Drax's worst nightmare was unfolding. He had faced Ronan and had been ignored!

Drax wasn't about to let Ronan get away. With the villain's back turned, Drax raised his knives and ran at him with a roar. But just before his blade could bite through Ronan's armor, the Accuser spun and Drax skidded by. He struck again, and Ronan parried. He struck again and Ronan punched back, as hard as Drax had ever been hit. He hurtled away and smashed into a steel doorway nearby.

Drax got up. He wasn't done yet. Ronan would answer for his crimes.

Several of Ronan's Sakaaran soldiers flew their Necrocraft in pursuit of the much slower mining pods that Gamora, Rocket, and Peter were trying to escape in. But it quickly became clear that their main focus was Gamora. Since she was drawing their fire, Peter knew it was up to him and Rocket to try to deal with the ships. "Rocket, keep them off Gamora until she gets to the *Milano*!"

"How? We've got no weaponry on these things!"

"These pods are industrial grade," Peter shouted to Rocket over the pod's communicator. "They're nearly indestructible."

"Not against Necro-blasts, they're not!" warned Rocket.

"That's not what I'm saying," said Peter.

"Oh..." said Rocket. Seeing Peter's meaning, Rocket turned his pod on a dime and smashed it right into one of the Necrocraft pursuing Gamora. The ship tumbled into another, and both crashed into mining platforms, destroying them in storms of flame and debris. The pod rocked and spun from the impact. When Rocket got it under control, he was facing another Necrocraft, powering up its blaster. He slammed the thrusters to max and smashed into the Necrocraft, shattering it and driving straight through—and all the while yelling like a maniac.

They weren't getting enough of the Necrocraft off

Gamora's tail, though. Peter had another idea. He flew his own pod close over the top of another of the Necrocraft and matched its speed. Then he deployed the mining pod's heavy pincer arms. They were usually used to pick up heavy crates or large chunks of ore, but they worked well for tearing the top off a Necrocraft, too.

"Let me borrow your ride!" Peter said to the pilot as he sucked him out through the hole in the Necrocraft's cockpit roof. Then Peter nestled his pod into the hole and used its pincer arms to control the Necrocraft. Before Ronan's minions knew what had happened, Peter had already flamed three of them. It was a good start, but Gamora still had at least that many on her tail. *Guess I'll have to shoot faster*, Peter thought. He wheeled around and kept chasing.

But that's when Peter got a transmission from Gamora. Pursuing Necrocraft had her trapped against one of the bone walls at the edge of Knowhere. He could hear her bouncing and skidding along it, grunting with effort as she tried to keep control over her pod.

"Quill! I'm trapped! I can't make it to the *Milano*!" she called. "I'll have to head up!" She steered her pod straight out through one of Knowhere's eyeholes and into open space. The Necrocraft stayed tight on her tail.

"What...? Wait!" shouted Peter. "Those things aren't meant to go out there!" The mining pods weren't equipped to operate outside Knowhere. They didn't have good life support and it was harder to maneuver them in a vacuum.

Over the Necrocraft's communication link, he heard Nebula's voice. "You are a disappointment, sister. Of all our siblings, I hated you least."

Geez, Peter thought to himself. *And I thought I had family issues.* Now he knew who Ronan had put in charge of capturing Gamora, too.

Pulling himself up, Drax made another run at Ronan, but Ronan caught him around the neck. Drax hammered punches into Ronan's midsection, but Ronan barely flinched. He squeezed, and Drax grunted with pain. Then Ronan lifted him up and slammed him into the ground so hard that Drax couldn't get up. He couldn't breathe.

Ronan looked down at Drax. "I don't recall killing your family," he said with no emotion. "I doubt I will recall killing you, either."

With that he hurled Drax into one of the nearby yellow pools of waste chemicals by the side of the road.

"Nebula, please," Gamora said as the Necrocraft chased her pod farther from Knowhere. "If Ronan gets this Stone, he'll kill us all!"

"Not all, sister," sneered Nebula. "You'll already be dead."

Her next shot destroyed the rear of Gamora's pod, and the pod disintegrated, leaving Gamora's body drifting in the void. As Peter watched, stunned, Nebula locked the Orb in a tractor beam and drew it into her Necrocraft. Then she and Ronan's other pilots flew away in formation, headed for a rendezvous with Ronan...and Thanos.

As Ronan walked away from Drax, he got a call on his communicator. "Ronan, it is done," said Nebula. Ronan smiled as his landing ship hovered into position behind him. He would meet her back at the *Dark Aster*, and the Orb would be his.

Peter, from inside his pod, stared helplessly at Gamora's floating body. She wouldn't be able to last out there for long!

"Quill! Come on," Rocket said quietly from his pod as it drifted up next to Peter's. "Her body mods should keep her alive for a couple more minutes, but there's nothing we can do for her. These pods aren't meant to be out here. In a second, we're gonna be in the same boat."

Rocket steered his pod back toward Knowhere. But Peter couldn't bear to leave Gamora drifting. The problem was, he didn't have a good idea of how to do anything about it.

He did, however, have a bad idea.

"Yondu, are you there? This is Quill!" said Peter, tuning his communicator to a frequency often used by the Ravagers. "I'm at coordinates 227-k32-4, right outside Knowhere," continued Peter. "If you're here, come and get me. I'm all yours!"

"Quill! What are you doing?" shouted Rocket to Peter over the radio. "Whatever you do, don't—" But, cutting the radio, Peter didn't hear the end of Rocket's sentence. He was too busy doing the exact thing that Rocket was telling him not to do.

He took a deep breath and activated the device that created his red-goggled face mask. When it was in place, Peter cycled open the door to his mining pod, letting the air inside rush out into the void of space. Then he leaped from the pod, shooting off his boot rockets, and headed straight for Gamora.

Gamora's race was tough, their bodies strong—and she had been augmented with biotechnology that was almost superpowered. But even Gamora couldn't withstand the vacuum of space for very long. When Peter reached her, he could see that her skin was starting to crack. There was no question...she was almost gone.

Seeing all this, Rocket was horrified. "Quill, don't be ridiculous! You can't fit two people in there! You're going to die! You'll die in seconds! Quill! Quill!!!"

Peter touched the earpiece controlling his mask. It disappeared, exposing his face to the vacuum. Immediately he felt the burning in his eyes and on his skin as they started to freeze. He put the earpiece behind Gamora's ear and touched it. His Star-Lord mask built itself around her face...and a moment later she gasped. She was alive.

But he wouldn't be for long.

Peter could already feel himself going numb. He looked into Gamora's face. There were so many things that Peter had wanted to do in this universe and so many things he had wanted to see. He regretted those undone things, but he was a little surprised to realize that he didn't regret trying to save Gamora. Somehow, putting someone else first, even if it meant dying, felt good to him in a way that he never expected it would. Too bad he wouldn't live long enough to do it again.

He was drifting into unconsciousness, his brain shutting down from lack of oxygen, when Yondu and the Ravagers arrived.

CHAPTER 10

Peter hacked and wheezed himself back into consciousness on a steel floor. It was cold. Part of him knew that Yondu would soon be there to yell terrible things at him, and possibly do even worse things. But he saw Gamora's face. He saw her breathing. *Yes!* he thought. *I did something different. I made this happen.*

He had saved both of their lives...at least for the moment. His last-minute gamble on Yondu's need for revenge had worked! Now he just needed to figure out a way to turn Yondu's fury against him.

Gamora coughed herself awake next to him. "Quill...what happened?" she asked. Their faces were very close together. As close as they had been when she pulled a knife on him back in the bar in Knowhere.

"I saw you out there," Peter gasped. He was still getting his breath back. "I don't know what came over me...but I couldn't let you die. I found something inside myself. Something incredibly heroic. I mean, not to brag..."

Gamora rolled her eyes. The moment was gone, and as usual Peter was too caught up in himself to think about anything else. "Where's the Orb?" she said with a sigh.

He hesitated. "It's...well...they got the Orb."

Her eyes widened and she started to sit up. "What?"

Right then, before she could get too mad at him, a group of Yondu's Ravagers piled into the tractor-beam receiving lock. "Welcome home, Peter," one of them said.

Back outside the Collector's destroyed museum inside Knowhere, Drax's limp body sank to the bottom of the fetid yellow pool—until two leafy tendrils reached down and wrapped themselves around him. Groot pulled Drax to the surface, sliding his body onto dry land. He looked down at Drax, and you could almost see him figuring out what was wrong. Drax had lungs and metabolized air. He'd been under the surface of a fluid. Therefore...

Groot extruded a long thorn from one of his fingers and punched a hole through Drax's chest, about where he thought the lungs must be. A spout of yellow fluid shot up in the air and Drax sat up, sputtering and gagging up more of the fluid. Groot withdrew the thorn and helped Drax start to get up. While Drax was still heaving up more yellow goo, Rocket came crashing down in one of the mining pods and opened the door.

"Blasted idiot!" Rocket shouted, jumping out and stomping toward Drax, who was just barely able to sit up. "I'm surrounded by idiots! Quill just got himself captured! And none of this would have happened if you didn't try to single-handedly take on a whole army!"

Still recovering, Drax did the last thing Rocket or Groot would have expected. He nodded. "You're right. I was a fool. All my anger...all my rage...was just to cover my loss."

Groot laid a hand on Drax's shoulder in sympathy, but Rocket wasn't done yet. "'Oh, boo-hoo-hoo. My wife and child are dead....'" ranted Rocket.

Groot covered his mouth in shock at Rocket's insensitive comments. Rocket looked at him. "I don't care if it's mean. Everybody's got dead people. It's no excuse to get everybody else dead along the way!"

Drax thought about this as Rocket stood up straight and turned to walk away. "Come on, Groot. Ronan has the Orb now. The only chance we have is to get to the other side of the universe as fast as we can, and maybe, just maybe, we'll be able to live full lives before that wack job ever gets there."

But Groot didn't follow Rocket. He stood, drawing himself up to his full height. "I am Groot."

"Save them? How?"

"I am Groot!"

"I know they're the only friends we've ever had," responded Rocket. "But there's an army of Ravagers around them and there's only two of us!"

"Three," said Drax, who was just now getting to his feet. He slapped a hand on to Groot's back, and both of them looked at Rocket.

He lost his temper, but not at anything in particular. With a frustrated growl, he turned and started kicking a tuft of wild grass growing near the pool of yellow fluid.

With each kick he barked out a word. "You're making me...beat...up...grass!"

Drax and Groot waited for him to get it out of his system so they could start to make a plan.

Aboard the *Dark Aster*, Ronan stood waiting for Thanos to appear on the wall of his consultation chamber. Next to him, Korath held the Orb. He saw the visage of the Mad Titan and he got started.

"The Orb is in my possession," he proclaimed. "As I promised."

"Bring it to me," Thanos said immediately, also not bothering with pleasantries.

"Yes," Ronan said, taking the talisman. "That was our agreement. Bring you the Orb and you will destroy Xandar for me. However, now that I know it contains an Infinity Stone, I wonder what use I have for you."

Thanos bared his teeth. "Boy, I would reconsider your present course."

But Ronan was too busy twisting open the Orb to notice. The purple light of the Infinity Stone lanced out through the interior of the *Dark Aster*.

"Master! You cannot!" Korath warned. "Thanos is the most powerful being in the universe!"

"Not anymore," Ronan said, and closed his fist around the Infinity Stone. He flung his head back and screamed with the pain and effort of containing its energies. With his other hand he reached out and took the Cosmi-Rod from the terrified Korath. He slammed the Infinity Stone into the hammer head of the Cosmi-Rod, and its violet radiance glowed from the hammer and also from Ronan's own body.

From her customary spot at the side of the hall, where few would notice her presence, Nebula watched. Ronan turned back to the wall displaying Thanos's face. "You call me boy," he growled. "I will unfurl one thousand years of Kree justice on Xandar, and burn it to its core! Then, Thanos..." Ronan's eyes flashed the same purple as the Infinity Stone. "I am coming for you."

"After Xandar, you are going to kill my father?" Nebula asked when Ronan had ended the consultation and turned away from the blank wall.

He looked her up and down. "You dare to oppose me?"

"You see what he has turned me into," she said, her voice low and hot with anger. "You kill him, and I will help you to destroy a thousand planets."

On board the Ravager ship, Peter took another brutal hit to his stomach. "You betray me!?" Yondu raged. He hit Peter again. "Steal my money!?" The Ravagers laughed. Many of them didn't like Peter. They thought he'd gotten special treatment when he was a boy, and now they loved seeing him on Yondu's bad side. Peter's head drooped. He'd taken a terrible beating already, and it was only going to get worse.

"Stop it!" shouted Gamora. Several strong Ravagers held her back. "Leave him alone!"

"When I picked you up, these boys wanted to eat you! They ain't never tasted Terran before. I saved your life!"

Peter straightened up and looked Yondu in the eyes. "Oh, will you shut up about that? Twenty years you've been throwing that in my face. Like it's some great thing, not eating me! Normal people don't even think about eating someone else, much less that person having to be grateful for it! You abducted me, man! You stole me from my home and from my family!"

"You don't give a damn about your Terra!" Yondu shouted. "You're scared because you're soft in here!" He pounded his fists on his own chest, then on Peter's. "Right here!"

"Yondu, listen to me!" Gamora strained against the goons holding her. "Ronan has something called an Infinity Stone."

"I know what he's got, girl," Yondu said. He looked back toward Peter.

"Then you know we must get it back. He's going to use it to wipe out Xandar. We have to warn them," Gamora said, changing her tone. "Billions of people will perish."

"Is that what she's been filling your head with, boy?" Yondu asked Peter. "Sentiment!" He slapped Peter square in the face. "Eating away your brain like maggots!"

He stepped back, shaking his head in disappointment. More quietly Yondu said, "That's it," and whistled. The steel arrow, already glowing red-hot, leaped from his belt to hover just a fraction of an inch from Peter's throat.

"Sorry, boy," Yondu said over the laughter of his Ravagers, "but a captain's got to teach his men what happens to those who cross him."

"Captain's gotta teach stuff!" another of the Ravagers shouted. They all loudly agreed. Through the growing noise came the clear sound of Peter's voice.

"If you kill me now, you are saying good-bye to the biggest score you have ever seen."

That comment stopped all of the outlaws in their tracks. But Yondu knew Peter was playing some kind of game. He kept the arrow right where it was and turned to face Peter again. "The Stone?" he said. "I hope you got something better than that, 'cause ain't nobody stealing from Ronan."

"We got a ringer," Peter said, and cut his eyes at Gamora.

Yondu didn't follow Peter's gaze, but he knew who Peter was looking at. "Is that right?"

"She knows everything there is to know about Ronan," Peter said. "His ships, his army..."

"He's vulnerable," Gamora said, taking her cue.

"What do you say, Yondu?" Peter asked. It cramped his style a little to have a superheated metal arrow so close to his throat, but he made things work. "Me and you, taking down a mark side by side, like the old days."

Yondu stared into Peter's face for a long moment. Then he whistled the steel arrow back into its sheath and shouted out a laugh. "Let 'em go!" he ordered. "You always did have guts, boy! That's why I kept you on as a young'un!"

Gamora jerked herself free of the Ravagers holding her and pinned each of them with a glare that promised death if they ever touched her again.

The Ravager ship shifted gears. One minute they were ready for an execution, the next they were ready to party—and then a minute after that, the ship shook with a small explosion. Yondu ran for the bridge. Peter and Gamora were right behind him.

Out the bridge window, Peter saw the incredible—and incredibly welcome!—sight of his very own ship, the *Milano*. A moment later he heard the unmistakable voice of Rocket Raccoon.

But before Peter could answer, a communication screen burst to life. "Attention, idiots!" said Rocket on the screen. "The lunatic on top of this ship is holding a Hadron Enforcer, a weapon of my own design."

"What the hell...?" Yondu said. He was amazed to see a tiny animal at the controls of the ship issuing threats.

"If you don't hand over our companions now," Rocket went on, "he's going to tear your ship apart!"

"I ain't buyin' it," Yondu said.

"I'm giving you to the count of five. Five..."

Chaos erupted on the Ravager ship's bridge. They could all see someone in a space suit standing on top of the *Milano* with some kind of weapon. Only Peter knew it was Drax, and even he didn't know what a Hadron Enforcer might be.

"Four," Rocket said. "Three..."

Peter ran to the communicator screen. "No, wait!" he shouted over the cacophony. "Rocket, it's me! We're fine. We've worked it out!"

Rocket's whole demeanor changed. "Oh, hey, Quill. What's going on?"

Ten minutes later, they were all on board the *Milano*, and of course they started arguing immediately. "You call that figuring it out?" Rocket said when he heard Peter's plan. "We're gonna rob the guys who beat us senseless?"

"You want to talk about senseless?" Peter shot back. "How about trying to save us by blowing us up?"

"We were only going to blow you up if they didn't turn you over!" Rocket said, like it was the most obvious thing in the world.

"And how on earth were they going to turn us over when you only gave them until a count of five?"

"We didn't have time to work out all the minutiae of the plan," Rocket said. "This is what we get for acting altruistically."

"I am Groot," Groot said.

"They are ungrateful," agreed Rocket, sullen.

Gamora had had enough of the bickering. "What's important now is we get the Ravagers' army to help us save Xandar."

"So we can give the Stone to Xandar, who's just going to sell it to somebody worse?" Rocket countered.

"We'll figure that part out later," Peter said.

"We have to stop Ronan," Gamora insisted.

"How?" Rocket threw up his hands.

"I have a plan," Peter said.

"You've got a plan," Rocket echoed, clearly not believing it.

"Yes."

"First of all, you're copying me from when I said I had a plan."

"No, I'm not," Peter said. "People say that all the time. It's not that unique of a thing to say."

"Secondly," Rocket went on, "I don't even believe you have a plan."

"I have ... part of a plan," Peter said.

"What percentage of a plan do you have?" Drax asked.

Gamora pointed an accusing finger at him. "You don't get to ask questions after the nonsense you pulled on Knowhere."

"I just saved Quill," Drax pointed out.

"We've already established that you destroying the ship that I'm on is not saving me," Peter argued.

"When did we establish it?" Drax said.

"Like three seconds ago!" Peter yelled.

"I wasn't listening. I was thinking of something else."

Gamora groaned and rolled her eyes.

"She's right," Rocket said to Drax. "You don't get an opinion." He turned back to Peter. "What percentage?"

"I don't know." Peter shrugged. "Twelve percent."

"Twelve percent?" Rocket burst out laughing.

"That's a fake laugh," Peter accused him.

"It's real," Rocket said.

"Totally fake."

"That is the most real, authentic hysterical laugh of my entire life because that is not a plan," Rocket said.

"It's barely a concept," Gamora agreed.

Peter gaped at her. "You're taking their side?"

"I am Groot," said Groot.

"So what if it's better than eleven percent?" Rocket said disbelievingly. "What the hell does that have to do with anything?"

"Thank you, Groot," Peter said, and chucked his massive treelike pal on the shoulder. "See? Groot's the only one of you who has a clue." He shifted his tone, dropping his voice and trying to bring them all together instead of continuing the argument. "Guys, come on. Yondu is going to be here in like two seconds. He expects to hear this big plan of ours. I need your help."

They all just stared at him.

"I look around at us, and you know what I see? Losers," Peter went on. He paused. That hadn't come out like he'd meant it to. "I mean, like, people who have lost stuff. And we have, man, we have. All of us. Our homes, our families, normal lives. Usually life takes more than it gives, but not today. Today it has given us something. It has given us a chance."

"To do what?" Drax asked.

"To give a damn. For once. To not run away," Peter said. "I for one am not going to stand by and watch as Ronan wipes out billions of innocent lives."

"But, Quill," said a dejected Rocket. "Stopping Ronan... it's impossible. You're asking us to die."

Peter considered this, and after a pause he said, "Yeah, I guess I am." He wasn't sure what else to add. Shaking his head, he took a few aimless steps away from where the rest of the group sat in a circle.

For a long moment there was silence aboard the *Milano*. Then Gamora said, "Quill."

He turned to look at her.

"I have lived most of my life surrounded by my enemies," she said. Then she stood. "I will be grateful to die among my friends."

Drax stood, too, as Peter took a step back toward the group. "You are an honorable man, Quill. I will fight beside you." Drax smiled. It was a thin smile, but even so, it was the first real smile Peter had ever seen on his face. "And in the end, I will see my wife and daughter again."

Groot stood, towering over the rest of them. "I am Groot," he said slowly.

They all looked at Rocket, who looked back at each of them in turn. His shoulders slumped and he sighed. "I don't got that long a life-span anyway," he said.

He stood on his stool so he was closer to the height of the rest of the group. "Now I'm standing," he said. "You happy? We're all standing up now."

CHAPTER 11

They got down to work, to the sounds of Awesome Mix Tape Vol. 1. Yondu and his chief lieutenant Kraglin arrived aboard the *Milano* and Peter nodded to Gamora to start things off with a little background. "The Stone reacts to anything organic," Gamora said. She'd learned some of its lore during her time with Thanos. "The bigger the target, the bigger the power surge."

"All Ronan's got to do is touch the Stone to the planet's surface, and zap," Peter said. "All plants, animals, Nova Corps…"

"Everything will die," Gamora summed up.

"So Ronan does not make the surface," Peter said. That was the linchpin of their plan, keeping the Accuser from getting the Infinity Stone down to the surface of Xandar. It was really their only chance.

"Rocket will lead a team to blow a hole in the *Dark Aster*'s starboard hull," Peter said. One of the display screens in the *Milano*'s common area showed a simulation as he outlined the plan. "Then our craft and Yondu's will enter."

"Won't there be hundreds of Sakaaran soldiers inside?" asked Kraglin.

"I think of Sakaarans as paper people," Drax said. Kraglin grinned and gave him a friendly punch on the arm.

Drax turned on him, ready to fight. Kraglin backed away. Drax didn't push it. He knew people sometimes did things they didn't mean, but he was still having trouble understanding how or why.

"Once we're on board," Gamora said, picking up where Peter had left off, "Ronan will isolate himself behind impenetrable security doors on deck . . . which I can disable by dismantling the power source."

"We'll make it to the flight deck, and I'll use the Hadron Enforcer to take Ronan out," Peter added.

"Once Ronan is dead, we will retrieve the Stone. Use these devices to contain it," Gamora instructed, as a

Ravager went around the room handing out copies of the Orb—which they all now knew was just a carrying case. "If you touch it," she added, "it will kill you."

"I'll contact one of the Nova officers who arrested us," Peter said. "Hopefully they'll believe we're there to help." He was thinking of Corpsman Dey. They had a history and, well, it wasn't all bad.

"There's one more thing we need to complete the plan," Rocket interrupted. He pointed at one of the Ravagers, a long-haired mountain of a man with a cybernetic implant covering part of his face. "That guy's eye."

"No, no we don't," Peter said before Rocket's joke could get them all in trouble the way it almost had back in the Kyln. "We don't need that guy's eye."

"No, seriously, I need it!" Rocket said. "It's important to me—" Then he started to giggle. Peter hustled him back down to the armory. It was time for all of them to get ready.

An hour or so later, they were. Rocket had his four-barreled favorite rifle. Drax had knives sheathed along both legs. Gamora wore a jumpsuit she'd made herself with help from the ship's onboard workshop, with a variety of blades stowed in various sheaths and pockets. Groot had grown spiky. And Peter? He checked over his mask and boot jets, his blasters...he was ready to go. Because all of his spare materials were dark red synthetic leather, that's what all of them were wearing. It so happened that the color went well with the highlights in Gamora's hair.

"Ronan's fleet has been spotted," one of the Ravagers reported from Yondu's ship. "Arrival in T-minus fifteen minutes."

Yondu caught up with Peter as they made their final preparations. "Remember, boy. At the end of all this, I get the Stone. You cross me, we kill you all."

Peter nodded at him and walked away. That was the part of the plan he hadn't quite figured out yet.

When it was time to go, Yondu called out, "Let's go get 'em, boys!" A squadron of Ravager fighters dropped out of the belly bay of Yondu's ship, streaking toward the *Dark Aster* through the upper reaches of Xandar's atmosphere.

The *Milano* flew with them, near the side of their formation. "This is a terrible plan," Gamora groused from the copilot's chair.

"Hey, you're the one who said you wanted to die among friends," Peter joked. He was riding high now that they were committed. The only thing to do was plunge ahead and see if they could make it work.

On the surface of Xandar, in the Nova Corps command center, Corpsman Dey approached Nova Prime, who was monitoring an unidentified fleet of small spacecraft within Xandarian space. "Nova Prime," he said. "I've received a transmission from one of the Ravagers. He says Ronan is in possession of something called an Infinity Stone and he's headed toward Xandar."

"Good God," Nova Prime said.

"It's a trick," said Corpsman Saal from the other side of the operations table. "He's a criminal."

"Did he say why we should believe him?" Nova Prime asked Dey.

"He said he and his crew just escaped from prison, so he'd have no other reason to risk coming to Xandar to help," Dey said. "He said that he's a...crook...but not, and I'm quoting here, one hundred percent a jerk."

Nova Prime digested this. "Do you believe him?"

"Well, I don't know that I believe anyone's one hundred percent a jerk, ma'am," Dey said.

Exasperated, she said, "I mean, do you believe that he is here to help?"

Dey paused. There was a lot riding on his answer. But he went with his gut. He knew Peter Quill. Rapscallion, thief, outlaw...yes. But Dey thought Quill was on the whole a decent guy.

"Yeah," he said.

CHAPTER 12

The *Dark Aster*'s hull glowed with the heat of reentry as it descended into the high atmosphere of Xandar. In his throne room, Ronan sat and waited for his moment. In a short time, Xandar would be destroyed and he would reign unchallenged as the greatest power in the galaxy. Not even Thanos would dare to oppose him now that he possessed one of the Infinity Stones.

Nebula appeared before him. He had not noticed her because he was lost in thoughts of his conquest. "A fleet approaches," she said. "They appear to be Ravagers."

Ronan waved, and the far wall of the throne room became transparent. He and Nebula saw the approaching craft. What could they be planning? Surely they did not think a squadron of small fighters could destroy a ship as large and powerful as the *Dark Aster*?

Two of the Ravager craft, in the lead, fired plasma torpedoes. Nebula watched them approach, and then all she could see was the fiery wash of their explosion. The *Dark Aster*'s shielding had stopped the torpedoes, but while they burned themselves out, the ship was effectively blind.

When the plasma fires dissipated, she saw the last of the Ravager fleet—flying underneath the *Dark Aster*.

"All pilots, dive!" she commanded over the common frequency. "They're beneath us!"

Hundreds of Necrocraft buzzed out of the *Dark Aster*'s launch ports as Rocket and two Ravagers hovered near the chosen point on the *Dark Aster*'s hull. They concentrated their fire, hoping that the ship had not shifted its shields— and it hadn't! Their fire started to chew a hole through the hull, but they didn't have much time.

Below, on the surface, Nova Prime issued evacuation orders. Rocket heard the order go out over civil-defense channels. The *Dark Aster* started to move forward and drop toward the capital city of Xandar. He and the two Ravagers shifted to keep their ships' guns trained on the same spot.

Finally they found a weak spot, and a huge hole exploded open in the lower starboard part of the *Dark Aster's* hull. "Quill! Yondu! Now!" Rocket shouted.

Peter was dodging Necrocraft with Yondu as his wingman. They shot their way through Ronan's fleet, but it was tough. There were a lot of Necrocraft, more than the Ravagers would be able to shoot down. If they couldn't get inside the ship as Peter had planned, there was no way they would be able to save Xandar—wherever its people evacuated to.

A crippled Necrocraft crashed into the starboard wing of Yondu's ship, destroying the engine on that side and sending his ship spinning out of control. "I'm goin' down, Quill! No more games, boy! I'll see you at the end of this!" he shouted.

His ship spiraled downward toward the surface, trailing smoke and pieces of its wing.

Peter's ship was taking fire, too. "There are too many

of them, Rocket!" Gamora cried out. "We'll never make it up there!"

But before Rocket could answer, the Necrocraft around them were blasted out of the sky. Craning their necks, Peter, Gamora, Drax, and Groot looked to see what had happened.

A tight formation of star-shaped Nova Corps fighters, gleaming gold in the Xandarian sun, moved into escort position. "Peter Quill," came a voice from the nearest. "This is Denarian Saal, of the Nova Corps. For the record, I advised against trusting you here."

"They got my jerk message!" Peter exulted.

"Prove me wrong," Saal said, and peeled away to rejoin the battle.

Peter's heart jumped. His message to Corpsman Dey had paid off! The Nova Corps had decided to trust them.

Now they needed to repay that trust.

He rammed the *Milano*'s thrusters to max and arrowed through the space between them and the *Dark Aster*, crashing through the hole Rocket had made and bouncing through the ship's interior. Sakaaran soldiers deployed in the hangar immediately started firing at them as Drax laughed uncontrollably from the rear cockpit seat.

"Yes!" he roared, raising his arms like a kid on a roller coaster.

Peter hauled the *Milano* into a sideways skid, opening fire on the Sakaarans. The *Milano*'s guns were designed to destroy small spaceships. They had no problem tearing the Sakaaran forces apart. By the time the ship came to rest, with Drax still laughing like a maniac, the Sakaarans were retreating, and they had a moment to get out of the ship without taking fire.

"The starboard kern has been breached!" Nebula reported. "We have been boarded!"

Around them, the *Dark Aster*'s wings were shifting and reconfiguring themselves. Ronan saw the approaching Nova Corps, and he knew how to deal with them. "Continue our approach," he ordered.

"But the Nova Corps have engaged!" she protested.

"None of that will matter once we reach the surface."

Nebula decided she would have to take the boarding into her own hands. "Seal security doors!" she ordered as she strode out of the throne room. She repeated the command in Sakaaran. The doors slammed shut behind her.

In the Nova Corps command center, Nova Prime tracked the *Dark Aster* as it descended toward the city. "All Nova pilots, interlock and form a blockade," she ordered. "The *Dark Aster* must not reach the ground."

Two hundred or more Nova Corps fighters aligned themselves in front of the *Dark Aster* in a formation that looked like a net. Energy crackled from the points of their longer wings, and they became an interconnected defense shield. "Locked in," they reported one after another as the shield filled out and became a glowing golden net a mile wide, waiting to catch the *Dark Aster*. Necrocraft bounced away from it in flames, and the *Dark Aster* loomed closer. It touched the blockade, and its immense mass pushed in... but the blockade held as the Nova Corps pilots fired their engines to full capacity. None of them could have stopped it on their own, but working together they arrested the *Dark Aster*'s progress toward the surface... at least for the moment.

Inside the *Dark Aster*, Peter led Gamora, Groot, and Drax into an area where the power had been cut off from explosive damage. "I can barely see," Drax said.

Groot raised one hand and hundreds—no, thousands—of glowing spores floated away from it, bathing the hangar in a bioluminescent glow. Peter was fascinated by the sight. It reminded him of fireflies back on Earth. "When did you learn to do that?" Drax asked Groot.

"I'm pretty sure the answer is 'I am Groot,'" Peter said.

Gamora peered ahead. "The flight deck is three hundred meters this way," she said, pointing. They moved ahead, through the drifting spores. It was a moment of strange beauty in the middle of the battle being fought around them.

"I want you to know that I am grateful for your acceptance after my blunders," Drax said. "It is pleasing to once again have...friends. You, Quill, are my friend."

"Thanks," Peter said.

"This dumb tree, he is my friend."

Groot grunted.

"And this green murderess, she, too—"

Gamora spun around. "Oh, you must stop!"

Drax looked confused. He was only being literal, as always. But before he had a chance to say anything, the lithe blue form of Nebula dropped down from an upper level of the hangar, blocking their progress.

"Gamora, look at what you have done," she said. "You have always been weak. You stupid, traitorous—"

Drax interrupted her with a blast from the shoulder-fired cannon he was carrying. It knocked her out of sight into the darkness. As the echoes of the blast died away, he said, "Nobody talks to my friends like that."

Gamora looked at him, then back ahead. Peter wanted to ask her what kind of history she had with the blue woman. Clearly there was something personal there. But there wasn't time.

"Head to the flight deck," she said. "I'll shut down the power to the security doors."

She continued on, and the rest of them veered to the left. The flight deck wasn't far away.

On the ground, Yondu stood in the wreckage of his ship. He picked up one of his favorite little toys, the one he'd gotten at the Broker's office, and tucked it into an inside pocket of his coat. He'd survived the crash, but he wasn't feeling too well, and he was feeling a lot worse when he looked up to see himself surrounded by Sakaaran soldiers. Their ship hovered a hundred meters or so away.

"Yondu Udonta," ordered the Sakaaran commander. "Order your Ravagers to turn on the Nova Corps."

Yondu didn't answer. Instead he flipped back the right side of his coat and whistled.

There were about a dozen Sakaaran soldiers ringing him, plus a pilot waiting in the Necrocraft. At Yondu's whistle, the arrow flashed out of its sheath at his belt. Before any of the Sakaarans could react, it had shot through each and every one of them, killing them where they stood. For good measure, it punched through the hull of the Necrocraft, too, which crashed in a fireball just as the last Sakaaran soldier pitched over and lay still.

Nobody tells Yondu Udonta what to do with his Ravagers.

Gamora heard the sounds of bones cracking in the dimness ahead, and scraping sounds on the ground. As she got closer to the sounds, she saw that they came from Nebula. Cybernetically enhanced with the ability to repair just about any damage to her body, Nebula was already standing and recovering from the blast of Drax's rocket. As Gamora stopped short, Nebula worked her jaw back into place and drew a baton.

"Nebula, please," Gamora said—but Nebula attacked.

Gamora parried the baton strike and drove a knee into

Nebula's midsection, doubling her over. She then ran to the power column that controlled the security doors on the flight deck protecting Ronan's chamber. She pulled the power coil free, and was about to disable it when Nebula struck again. Now she had both of her batons out and fully extended. They carried a powerful electric charge, and the impact of the first one dropped Gamora to her knees.

She turned and fought back against her adopted sister, knowing that she was fighting for her life.

In his chamber, Ronan grew impatient with the slow progress against the Nova Corps shield. Even the *Dark Aster*'s powerful engines could not force the ship through the shield, and his weapons' energies were just absorbed uselessly into it. "Enough of this," he said. "Necrocraft, enact immolation initiative."

The Necrocraft peeled away and dove toward the city.

"They're dive-bombing the city!" one of the Nova Corps pilots called out over their common channel. "Denarian Saal, should we break formation?"

"No!" Saal ordered. "Hold your positions!"

Turning themselves into falling bombs, the Necro-craft exploded on impact throughout the city of Xandar. They destroyed buildings and started fires as terrified civilians fled. Nova Corps forces on the ground tried to shoot the Necrocraft out of the sky, but there were too many of them. One crashed into the same plaza where Peter, Gamora, Rocket, and Groot had all met just a few days before.

From the Nova Corps command center, Nova Prime watched helplessly as fires bloomed across the city—then she was given another moment of hope as the Ravagers swung low out of the smoky sky, blasting the next wave of Necrocraft to fragments before they could crash.

"Keep Ronan up there, Saal," Rocket said as he casually blew another Necrocraft apart. "We'll take care of the people down here."

He and the rest of the Ravagers flew low and hovered, noses pointing up. "Everybody shoot them before they hit the ground," Rocket said. The Ravagers opened fire. They didn't get all of the Necrocraft, but they got most of them. The city wouldn't be destroyed right away.

Nova Prime breathed a sigh of relief. Their defenses were holding. Barely, but they were holding.

On board the *Dark Aster*, Peter led Drax and Groot around a corner toward Ronan's chamber—and smack into a detachment of Sakaarans. And there, right up front, was Korath, who had nearly ended this whole adventure before it began, back on Morag.

"Star-Lord," Korath said with a menacing grin. The cybernetic assembly on his skull glowed the same color as his eyes, an electric blue.

Peter was thrilled to hear someone call him that. "Finally!" he said.

Then Korath broke the mood by tackling Peter and flinging him to the deck. He pounded on Peter, who managed to get his mask into place before Korath could ruin his good looks. But Korath was a lot stronger than Peter was, and he was also angry at how Peter had humiliated him before. "You thief!" Korath said. "You will never make it to Ronan!"

Drax cut down a number of Sakaaran soldiers and then threw a knife at Korath, who dodged it. Then Drax came charging to the rescue, but even he was overmatched by Korath's incredible strength. The Sakaaran leader met

Drax head-on and knocked him to the ground with a punch. Groot was flinging Sakaarans this way and that, but Korath stood unhurt. They were going to have to get through him one way or another.

Peter got his blasters in his hands. The fate of Xandar was at stake. He blazed away at the Sakaaran soldiers and Groot bashed them down as fast as he could get his hands on them. Meanwhile Drax and Korath were in a one-on-one struggle. Korath swung and cracked a stone pillar. Drax landed punches and threw Korath to the ground. Korath grappled with Drax, pounding away at him, but now Drax was fully into the heat of battle. He ignored Korath's blows and drove his foe into the wall.

Then he dragged a finger across Korath's throat in a clumsy imitation of what he had seen Peter do back on the Kyln. "Finger to the throat means death," he said. He grabbed on to the cybernetic assembly on Korath's head. He had figured out that it was linked into Korath's brain and gave him his strength and resistance to injury.

Drax squeezed, and sparks shot from the machine. Korath grunted and his eyes rolled back in his head. Drax squeezed harder and tore the machine free in a larger shower of sparks. Korath shut down. His body went limp and he slid down the wall and fell over on his side.

Drax turned to Peter, flush with his victory. "Metaphor," he said.

"Yeah, sorta," Peter said through his mask. Its red eyes glowed in the dim vaulted room. Then he saw more Sakaarans coming. "Oh, no."

Peter and Drax ran to meet this new threat, but before they could do anything about it Groot got there first. He extended one of his arms into a spiky vine, impaling a column of Sakaarans. With a loud roar, he lashed his viny arm back and forth, smashing the rest of the Sakaarans to the ground and then beating them until they weren't going to get up anymore. One last shake of the vine got rid of the Sakaarans stuck on his arm. He turned to look at Peter and Drax, and a big grin spread over his wooden face.

Peter and Drax grinned back. The security door was right in front of them. Now if only Gamora could get it open...

CHAPTER 13

Ronan stood as the *Dark Aster* drove into the Nova Corps shield. It was holding him back from his destiny, and he would no longer tolerate it. He opened a feed that would carry his voice to every speaker on the planet. "Xandar! You stand accused," he proclaimed. "Your wretched peace treaty will not save you now. It is the tinder on which you burn."

He raised the Cosmi-Rod and unleashed a ray of pure violet energy from the Infinity Stone. The Stone's energy overloaded the center of the Nova Corps' shield, incinerating thirty of their ships in an instant. The shield began to disintegrate as the overload spread from fighter to fighter. They burst into flames and fell from the sky.

The *Dark Aster*'s nose shoved through the hole in the Nova Corps shield, and then the rest of the ship followed. The Nova Corps fighters broke apart, falling away from the *Dark Aster*.

Nothing now stood between Ronan and the surface of Xandar.

"Quill, you gotta hurry," Rocket said. "The city's being evacuated, but we're getting our butts kicked down here."

"Gamora hasn't opened the door!" Peter answered as he shot the last Sakaaran out of the way. He pound on the door in frustration. Where was she?

A tumbling Nova Corps ship crashed into the *Dark Aster*'s hull, blasting a hole in it and scattering wreckage through the room where Gamora fought for her life. Her twin blades met Nebula's twin batons in a crackle and swirl of electricity. Wind from the outside howled. Nebula caught Gamora's blades and twisted them out of her hands, then jammed both of her batons into Gamora's torso. The discharge of electricity nearly brought Gamora to her knees again, but with a last desperate move she pivoted and kicked the batons from Nebula's hands.

Gamora scissored her legs, kicking again and knocking Nebula backward. Nebula lost her footing and slipped out the hole, sliding down the broken exterior and just barely catching a bent piece of plating with the spiked edge of her left wrist guard. Her feet kicked in the air, thousands of feet above the ground.

Nebula looked down to see if there was something she could grab on to, but there was nothing. She couldn't even work her left hand loose because her weight kept the wrist guard jammed in the broken plate. She was utterly helpless.

Then she heard Gamora call her name. She looked up to see Gamora leaning out the hole and reaching down. "Sister, help us fight Ronan. You know he's crazy!"

"I know you're both crazy," Nebula panted. She glanced down again, and saw a way out.

With a slash of her right-hand wrist blade, she severed her left hand above the guard and fell free and landed directly on the cockpit of a Ravager ship passing below. Nebula shattered the cockpit window and commandeered the ship, flying away and leaving Gamora to gaze after her in astonishment.

But she had little time to marvel. The entire planet

of Xandar was counting on her. She had to disarm those security doors.

Finding her knife, she hacked through the protective casing on the energy supply conduit and then chopped through enough of the wires that the doors were depowered. As the green glow of the conduit faded, Gamora picked up a gun and blasted a hole through the ceiling. Above was Ronan's chamber. She leaped up just as Peter and Drax and Groot came charging through the open door, blasting through Ronan's guards.

Peter saw Ronan, standing framed by the window at the other end of the chamber. The city of Xandar, smoke rising from a hundred fires, grew closer. Peter brought the Hadron Enforcer up, and before Ronan could react, he fired.

Hadrons were subatomic particles, and the way Rocket had explained the weapon, what it did was unleash the energy of those particles by breaking apart atoms in its target. It caused maybe a million, maybe a billion collisions— Rocket wasn't too sure—and each of them was powerful enough to put a hole in the armor of a ship.

The blast of the impact on Ronan shattered the walls of the room and the window beyond. Pieces fell from the ceiling and the four heroes almost lost their footing. The *Dark Aster* shook from the force of the explosion.

As the smoke cleared, Ronan was nowhere to be seen.

"You did it!" Drax said.

That's what Peter thought, too...for a moment.

Then Ronan stood up from the scattered debris. He didn't look hurt at all. But he did look angry.

He pointed the Cosmi-Rod at them and leveled them with a shock wave. Drax was the first to recover. He charged at Ronan, but Ronan caught him easily, lifting him off the ground and squeezing off his breath. Drax kicked and gasped as Ronan seemed to remember something. "I do remember your family," he said. "Their screams were—"

A rising noise cut him off and he looked out the fragmented window to see the looming shape of the *Milano*, coming in fast and not slowing down. Not one little bit. Peter, stunned and still getting back to his feet, caught a glimpse of Rocket in the cockpit. His teeth were bared and he held the thruster controls all the way forward.

The *Milano* slammed in through the window frame and hit Ronan and Drax first before smashing through the cyborgs who controlled the *Dark Aster*. Groot grabbed Peter and dove out of the way before the ship could crush them. It ground across the floor and came to rest against the back wall, near the open security door.

Explosions thundered through the room and the *Dark Aster* leaned forward and to the left, out of control. When the blasts subsided, Peter clambered up onto the *Milano*'s wing and tried to see if Rocket was all right. Groot watched from below. Gamora dragged the unconscious Drax up to them as Peter carried Rocket down. Around them, the ship shook and debris cascaded down from the ceiling. A wall collapsed somewhere nearby. The *Dark Aster* was starting to shake itself apart.

It fell faster now as it nosed fully downward. Fires burned around them. They were going to crash, and nothing in the galaxy could stop it.

A crackling noise reached their ears, and at first they thought it was a fire blazing up in the wrecked *Milano*. Then they looked around and saw that Groot was growing. Branches sprouted from his back and legs and shoulders, intertwining and reaching out around them. Hundreds of glowing spores floated among them as Groot created a sphere, wrapping them up in fresh growth. Leaves grew, and tiny flowers, and the branches kept getting thicker and tangling into more and more layers.

"No, Groot. You can't," Rocket said. He struggled free

of Peter and went to Groot, who was almost completely woven into the sphere. Only his head was still visible. "You'll die. Why are you doing this? Why?"

A tendril reached out and stroked the side of Rocket's muzzle. Somber and slow, Groot looked at each of his friends in turn and said, "We...are...Groot."

The *Dark Aster* crashed at the edge of Xandar's harbor, toppling buildings and tearing a trench a mile long through the city. A hundred explosions from different parts of the ship tore it completely to pieces, until the sliding wreckage came to rest on the Xandarian waterfront.

Near the remains of Groot, part of the *Milano* lay upright. The impact had shocked its stereo into life, and the first song on Awesome Mix Tape Vol. 1 was playing. "Things are gonna get easier..."

Drax twitched and raised one hand. A moment later, Gamora rolled over, groaning. Peter made similar sounds as he tried to sit up. All of them felt like they'd been put in a bag and pounded with hammers.

But they were alive. They were surrounded by a litter of broken branches and twigs, and they were alive.

Rocket knelt next to one pile of sticks. "I called him an idiot," he said, crying and holding a tiny sprig with a broken leaf at the end.

Xandarians started to approach them, amazed that such an apocalyptic crash had left any survivors. Peter saw the Broker look at the *Dark Aster*'s wreckage and shrink back. Around him, the other Xandarians did the same.

Peter turned and saw why.

Ronan, his hammer in hand, walked out of the smoking rubble. He walked slowly, looking around him at the scene. The Infinity Stone in the head of his hammer was less than two meters from the surface of Xandar.

For only the second time in his life, Peter felt hopeless.

"You killed Groot!" Rocket screamed. He charged at Ronan, who sent him flying with a flicker of energy from the hammer. Rocket pinwheeled across the crash site and slammed into a piece of the *Dark Aster*'s hull. He hit the ground and didn't get up.

"Behold!" Ronan called out. "Your guardians of the galaxy. What fruit have they wrought?"

Even in the desperate situation, Peter caught himself thinking how could fruit get wrought? Weird phrase. But Ronan was still talking, and they had bigger problems than word choice.

"Only that my father, and his father, shall finally know vengeance!" Ronan said.

Peter saw Rocket get to his feet, and was glad the little critter wasn't dead. Then he saw Rocket head for a piece of wreckage and start fiddling with it. What was he up to? Drax and Gamora saw it, too, but they stayed down. Rocket had found the Hadron Enforcer, and whatever he was doing, they didn't want Ronan to notice.

"People of Xandar, the time has come to rejoice and renounce your paltry gods!" Ronan raised the hammer overhead. "Your salvation is at hand!" He went on in the native language of the Kree—and that's when Peter realized he had to do something.

The song was still playing, and he got to his feet. He sang and danced his way up to Ronan. The Accuser lowered his hammer and looked at Peter incredulously.

"Listen to these words," Peter said. He kept singing, and as the song built to its bridge, he said, "Now bring it down hard!" He danced and sang and Ronan stared. So did Gamora and Drax, and everyone else who had gathered around. None of them had ever seen anything like it.

"What are you doing?" Ronan asked. At last Peter had found something that could break his concentration.

"Dance-off, bro!" Peter said. He kept grooving. "Me and you." He reached out to Gamora, inviting her to join. "Gamora."

She shook her head.

"Subtle," Peter said. He made a grabbing motion. "Take it back."

Ronan, over his initial shock, started to sound like Ronan again. "What are you doing?"

Peter grinned. "I'm distracting you, you big turd blossom!"

A ratcheting mechanical sound from Ronan's left drew his attention. It was Drax, racking the Hadron Enforcer into place. A split-second later, Rocket triggered it.

This time, they didn't aim at Ronan. That hadn't worked. This time, they zeroed the Hadron Enforcer right in on the Infinity Stone in the head of Ronan's hammer. The impact shattered the hammer's head, and the Infinity Stone flew free. Peter was already diving for it, and he got there a split-second before it hit the ground. He caught the Infinity Stone and cradled it into his body, keeping it from the surface of Xandar.

Its energy tore through him like nothing he'd ever experienced. He heard Gamora screaming, and he was screaming, too. He was at the center of a furious storm of violet energy that swirled around the crash site, walling in Rocket and Drax and Gamora with him...and with Ronan, who stood watching Peter, knowing that soon the energy of the Stone would tear him apart.

Peter held on by sheer willpower even as the power of the Infinity Stone surged through him. He felt like little pieces of himself were flying away into the storm, transformed into purple sparks that floated between him and his friends. The world started to fall away from him—or maybe that was him falling away from the world as the Infinity Stone started to disintegrate his mind.

Take my hand, someone said.

Peter saw his mother, reaching out. *Take my hand, Peter.*

He had failed her. He had held back and he'd spent the last twenty-six years wishing he could have that moment again and make it right.

Something shifted around him and he realized it wasn't his mother, it was Gamora, reaching out to help. "Take my hand!" she screamed over the storm.

He did. The Infinity Stone's energy scoured through her and she spasmed, feeling the same overwhelming power Peter had. Even the two of them weren't going to be able to contain it.

But a moment later a third joined them, as Drax struggled through the storm to clamp his hand on Peter's shoulder. His tattoos flared into the Infinity Stone's violet and he strained to keep the connection with Peter...but something had shifted. A moment before, Peter had been certain he was going to die. Now he had a glimmer of hope again—and when he looked down to see Rocket gripping his other hand, Peter understood something.

What none of them could do individually, all of them could do together. They stood linked together, the energy of the Infinity Stone still flooding them, but now they channeled it. They held it in check.

Astonished, Ronan looked on. "But...you're mortal," he said. "How?"

Peter, his eyes flaring violet—and maybe a little red, like the Infinity Stone had found something in him that he had never known was there—stared back at Ronan. "You said it yourself," he said. "We're the Guardians of the Galaxy."

He opened his hand and the power of the Infinity Stone lashed out, shattering Ronan's armor and lifting Ronan away from the ground. Just as it had done to the Collector's assistant, Carina, it flickered and strobed through

Ronan's body, transforming it into a burst of purple energy. Ronan cried out and disappeared in the flare, overwhelmed and destroyed by the very thing he had wanted above all else.

The moment of control wouldn't last. Even with Ronan gone, the Stone was still an incredible danger. Gamora slapped it into one of the new Orbs they all carried and the purple storm subsided, leaving only trailing breezes and a wisp of smoke where Ronan had stood a moment before.

"Well, well, well," came Yondu's voice in the aftermath. "Quite the light show. Ain't this sweet? But you got some business to attend to." The Ravagers accompanying him cocked their weapons.

"Peter, you can't," Gamora said as Yondu stepped down into the blasted circle.

"You gotta reconsider this, Yondu," Peter said. "I don't know who you're selling this to, but the only way the universe can survive is if you give it to the Nova Corps."

Yondu flipped his coat back. The metallic fin on his head started to glow, and so did the arrow. "I may be as pretty as an angel, but I sure ain't one," he said. He held out a hand. "Hand it over, son."

After a long pause, Peter brought the Orb out from behind his back. He dropped it in Yondu's palm.

Yondu chuckled and let his coat fall back into place. He gestured and the Ravagers started to head back to their ship. So did Yondu.

Peter called after him. "Yondu. Do not open that Orb. You've seen what it does to people."

Yondu pointed at him and gave him a wink. Then he headed for his ship. "Yeah, Quill turned out okay," Kraglin said as the Ravagers lifted off from Xandar. "Probably good we didn't deliver him to his dad like we was hired to do."

Peter and his friends watched the Ravagers go. "He is going to be so pissed when he finds out I switched the Orb on him," Peter said, bringing the real Orb out. All he'd had to do was swap Gamora's for his behind his back. Easiest thing in the world.

"He was going to kill you, Peter," Gamora said.

"Oh, I know," Peter said. "But he was about the only family I had."

Gamora clasped his hand that was holding the Orb. She made sure he was looking at her and said, "No. He wasn't."

Across the circle, Rocket sat sobbing over a tiny sprig of

Groot. Drax sat down next to him. Instead of speaking, he reached out and stroked the fur between Rocket's ears. Rocket startled. Then he relaxed and the two of them sat there mourning their lost friend. Xandar had been saved, but its salvation had come at a cost.

CHAPTER 14

In the aftermath, there were lots of loose ends to tie up. One of them had to do with criminal records. The Nova Corps officially pardoned all of them, but before they concluded their business, Corpsman Dey brought Peter and Gamora up to the Nova Corps command center. Peter felt a little nervous heading right into the thick of the police who had spent so much time chasing him, but hey. Things were different now.

They were even more different than he had suspected, as he found out when Nova Prime herself showed up and greeted him. "There's something we'd like you to see," she said, and Dey spawned a hologram medical dossier. Peter saw his name and image, and then a bunch of scientific gobbledygook. They got right down to business and told him something he couldn't believe at first.

"When we arrested you, we noticed an anomaly in your nervous system, so we had it checked out," Dey said.

Peter couldn't believe it. "I'm not Terran?"

"You're half-Terran," Nova Prime said. "Your mother was of Earth. Your father...well, he's something very ancient we've never seen here before."

"That could be why you were able to hold the Stone for as long as you did," Gamora speculated.

Bizarre, Peter thought. His mother had always said his father was an angel made of light...but what had he been really? Maybe one of these days he would find out.

A door opened and Peter saw Drax and Rocket enter. Rocket carried a pot of earth, with a stick stuck upright in it. Peter thought it was crazy, but Rocket had insisted, so they all went along with it.

"On behalf of the Nova Corps," Nova Prime said, "we would like to express our profound gratitude for your help in saving Xandar. If you will follow Denarian Dey, he has something to show you."

Denarian Dey, Peter thought. Good old Dey got himself a promotion. "Thank you, Nova Prime," he said.

Dey led them out of the command center. On the way, Gamora fell into step next to Drax. "Your wife and child will rest well knowing you have avenged them," she said.

"Yes," Drax said. "Of course, Ronan was only a puppet. It's really Thanos I need to kill."

She stopped and watched him go. Was he serious? Then she hurried to keep up with the rest of them, because Dey was already outside.

"We tried to keep it as close to the original as possible," Dey was saying as they came out onto the Nova Corps' rooftop flight pad. "We salvaged as much as we could."

Peter couldn't believe what he was seeing. The *Milano*, docked at the edge of the deck, looking as good as new. Better than new, maybe, Peter thought. He'd never seen it new because he'd kind of stolen it from Yondu. "Wow," he said. "Thank you."

"I have a family," Dey said. "They're alive because of you. Your criminal records have also been expunged," he added to Drax and Rocket, who hadn't been around for the first announcement. "However, I have to warn you against breaking any laws in the future."

"Question," Rocket said. "What if I see something I want to take and it belongs to someone else?"

"Then you will be arrested," Dey said.

"But what if I want it more than the person who has it?"

"It's still illegal."

"That doesn't follow. No, I want it more, sir," Rocket said. "Do you understand?"

Gamora chuckled quietly and started to guide Rocket toward the ship. "What are you laughing at?" he demanded. "What, I can't have a discussion with this gentleman?"

Drax had his own questions. "What if someone does something irksome and I decide to remove his spine?"

A little taken aback, Dey said, "That's actually…murder. One of the worst crimes of all. So, also illegal."

"Hmm," Drax said, as if this was the first time he'd ever heard that. He walked off to join Rocket and Gamora.

"They'll be fine, Dey," Peter assured him. "I'm gonna keep an eye on them."

"You?" Dey looked skeptical.

"Yeah. Me."

On the ship a little later, while Rocket was running the last preflight checks, Peter opened a drawer in the common area and found the present his mother had given him. He couldn't believe it had survived, but hey. Maybe he'd been wrong. Maybe life didn't always take more than it gave.

He opened the envelope attached to it and unfolded a note in his mother's hand.

Peter,

I know these last few months have been hard for you, but I'm going to a better place. And I will be okay. And I will always be with you. You are the light of my life. My precious son. My little Star-Lord.

Love, Mom

He read the note again, then set it aside and opened the package. Inside the small box, nestled in yellow tissue paper, was a cassette tape. Its label read Awesome Mix Tape Vol. 2.

A smile broke across Peter's face. He turned and clicked the tape into his stereo. There was a soft pop from when his mother had dropped the needle onto the record...and then the unmistakable intro to one of his mother's favorite songs.

Peter sat there, remembering how his mother had loved it. He let it wash over him a little. Then he looked up and saw Gamora watching him. She smiled at him, and then the music got to her, too. She started to groove. Just a little, but it was a start. He followed her up into the cockpit and strapped in next to Rocket. Drax was behind them.

In front of Rocket's seat, on the flight console, was his little flower pot. In it, the stick had already grown tiny arms and a face. It stretched, and a little leaf sprouted. Peter grinned.

"So," he said. "What should we do next? Something good? Something bad? A bit of both?"

"We'll follow your lead...Star-Lord," Gamora said. And she wasn't even joking.

"Bit of both," Peter said. Rocket gunned the engines and off they went, the Guardians of the Galaxy.

TURN THE PAGE FOR AN
EXCITING PREVIEW OF

MARVEL CINEMATIC UNIVERSE
PHASE ONE

MARVEL
THE AVENGERS

CHAPTER 1

Nick Fury should have been on the Helicarrier handling his responsibilities as director of S.H.I.E.L.D. The world was full of threats, and the Phase 2 defense initiative required all his attention. Instead, he was stepping off a helicopter in the New Mexico desert, with his right-hand agent, Maria Hill, right behind him.

Another of his most trusted agents, Phil Coulson, met them on the landing pad. The massive S.H.I.E.L.D.

research base loomed around them. It was a hive of activity, with low-level alarms sounding and an automated voice echoing over loudspeakers: *"All personnel, evacuation order has been confirmed. This is not a drill."*

"How bad is it?" Fury asked, raising his voice over the beating rotors of the helicopter.

"That's the problem, sir," Coulson said. "We don't know."

He got them up to speed as they rode the elevator down into the subterranean lab complex where S.H.I.E.L.D. had been housing the artifact known as the Tesseract. During World War II, Hydra had tried to use it to power doomsday weapons. Later, Tony Stark's father, Howard, one of S.H.I.E.L.D.'s founders, had recovered it. Ever since, S.H.I.E.L.D. had been trying to understand its secrets.

Last year, they had made a breakthrough with the assistance of Dr. Erik Selvig, an astrophysicist who had crossed paths with S.H.I.E.L.D. when his protégé Jane Foster had encountered a being from another world. The individual called himself Thor, after the thunder god of Norse mythology—and, after what had happened following Thor's arrival on Earth, Nick Fury believed he was legitimate. Whatever this being's true origin, he had a powerful hammer and he came from a place called Asgard...and he had formidable enemies who'd followed him to Earth.

Those enemies were gone, but Fury had learned his lesson. S.H.I.E.L.D. could no longer focus only on threats coming from Earth. They had to be ready for threats coming from anywhere in the universe.

That was why they'd brought Dr. Selvig in to study the Tesseract. If they could harness its power...

"Dr. Selvig read an energy surge from the Tesseract four hours ago," Coulson was saying.

"I didn't approve going to testing," Fury said.

Coulson nodded. "He wasn't testing it. He wasn't even in the room. Spontaneous event."

"It just turned itself on?" Hill sounded skeptical.

Fury, as usual, was less interested in how they'd gotten there than in what they were going to do next. "What are the energy levels now?"

"Climbing. When we couldn't shut it down, we ordered the evac," Coulson said.

"How long before we get everyone out?"

"Campus should be clear in the next half an hour."

"It better."

Fury and Maria Hill continued on toward the main research area. "Sir," she said as they walked, "evacuation may be futile."

"We should tell them to go back to sleep?"

"If we can't control the Tesseract's energy, there may not be a minimum safe distance."

"I need you to make sure the Phase Two prototypes are shipped out."

"Sir, is that really a priority right now?"

"Until such time as the world ends, we will act as though it intends to spin on. Clear out the tech below. Every piece of Phase Two on a truck and gone."

"Yes, sir." She took some agents with her and headed for the separate area where the Phase 2 prototypes were stored and tested.

Now Fury could focus on Erik Selvig. He stood surrounded by monitors and instruments designed to analyze the forces the Tesseract emitted. "Talk to me, Doctor," he said.

Selvig acknowledged him briefly and then returned his attention to the monitoring equipment. "Director, the Tesseract is misbehaving."

"Is that supposed to be funny?"

"No, it's not funny at all. The Tesseract is not only active, she's…*behaving*."

Fury didn't comment on the doctor characterizing the Tesseract as female. He also wasn't interested in Selvig's notions about its personality. It didn't have a personality. It was a cube containing energy, and all Nick Fury wanted was to know how to control that energy. "I assume you pulled the plug."

"She's an energy source. We turn off the power, she turns it back on. If she reaches peak level—"

"We prepared for this, Doctor. Harnessing energy from space."

"We're not ready. My calculations are far from complete. And she's throwing off interference radiation."

Fury watched the Tesseract in its circular containment shell. Eight separate energy sensors built into a frame supporting that shell were designed to measure and conduct that energy. Those sensors in turn rested on stainless-steel support scaffolding. The whole setup sprouted cables and conduits. These were there to supply energy to the Tesseract in a controlled fashion so Dr. Selvig could analyze its reactions. Now they were all shut down, as Dr. Selvig had said, but even so, the Tesseract glowed with a fierce blue energy. It was starting to spill onto the sensors, arcing like electricity. But it wasn't electricity. It was something much more exotic.

"Nothing harmful," Selvig assured him. "Low levels of gamma radiation."

Fury turned slowly to give him a look. "That can be harmful," he said softly. S.H.I.E.L.D. knew of at least one instance where gamma radiation had transformed an ordinary human being, Bruce Banner, into a practically indestructible monster, known as the Hulk. New York City was still recovering from the damage caused getting that one back under control.

"Where's Agent Barton?" he asked.

"The Hawk?" Selvig scoffed, getting Barton's nickname wrong. "In his nest, as usual." He pointed up.

Fury looked where he had pointed but didn't

see anything. "Agent Barton," he said into his mic, "report." All S.H.I.E.L.D. agents and assets wore miniature microphones at all times. Fury was a big believer in communications.

Hawkeye came sliding down a rope from the distant upper reaches of the lab space. When he got to the ground, Fury was already walking. Hawkeye followed. "I gave you this detail so you could keep a close eye on things," Fury said as they moved away from Selvig, leaving him to his work.

"Well, I see better from a distance."

"Have you seen anything that might set this thing off?"

"Doctors," a tech called from near them. "It's spiking again."

"No one's come or gone, and Selvig's clean," Hawkeye said. He and Fury mounted the platform holding the Tesseract's support structure as the cube crackled. "No contacts, no IMs. If there's any tampering, sir, it's not at this end."

Fury shot him a look. "At this end?"

"Yeah, the cube is a doorway to the other end of space, right? Doors open from both sides."

This was true, Fury thought. And he already knew that sometimes unwanted visitors came from space.

Behind him, Selvig cursed and pounded on his keyboard.

From the Tesseract came a fresh blast of energy. Everyone in the complex felt it. Those down in the lab could only watch as a vortex formed around the Tesseract, swirling and glowing. It tightened into a focused beam that shot across the length of the lab and blossomed into a sphere. The same blue energy roiled and sparked on the surface of the sphere. It grew, and the sound of the energy got louder. Inside it was a pure blackness, blotting out the test platform and railings where the sphere had appeared.

Something overloaded, and a wave of energy rolled out from it, flashing across the skin of Fury, Hawkeye, and the assembled scientists. They flinched, but they also wanted to see what was going on....

When the energy faded, a man was left on the platform. He was on one knee with his head tucked into his chest, as if riding out a storm. In the silence, they approached him. The energy blast had scattered equipment and materials across the floor.

The man looked up at them and smiled as he stood. He was not a large man, not remarkable in any particular way. He had long black hair and wore black leather clothing, similar to what Fury was wearing. However, he wasn't a S.H.I.E.L.D. agent. Fury didn't know where he had come from.

Also, the stranger held a kind of spear in his right hand. Set into its head, a gem glowed the same icy blue as the energy that had spilled from the Tesseract.

"Sir," Fury called as armed S.H.I.E.L.D. agents closed nearer, "please put down the spear."

The man looked at the scepter as if he had only just noticed he had it. Then, slowly, he looked back up at Fury, and a vicious smile spread across his face.

He jabbed the scepter in Fury's direction, and a blast of energy from it knocked Fury and Hawkeye back through a bank of monitors and instruments. The S.H.I.E.L.D. agents opened fire, but the bullets didn't seem to hurt the man. He leaped, scepter held high, and cut a path through the agents. In a very short time, the only people left standing in the lab were him and Hawkeye, who had just scrambled back to his feet. Before Hawkeye could unholster and aim his gun, this strange enemy was somehow already across the room. He caught Hawkeye's arm and said softly, "You have heart."

The tip of his scepter touched Hawkeye's chest, not hard enough to hurt him. The gem glowed, and a strange expression came over Hawkeye's face for a moment. He and the stranger looked each other in the eye, and Fury was amazed to see Hawkeye put his gun away.

Now Nick Fury really knew he was up against something...unusual. The only thing he could do was get the Tesseract and try to keep it safe while S.H.I.E.L.D. finished the evacuation and called in some special reinforcements. Tony had to hear about this.

Fury had the Tesseract in a steel carrying case and was taking a step toward the door when the stranger turned to him and said, "Please don't. I still need that."

"This doesn't have to get any messier," Fury said. He glanced quickly around, trying to figure the fastest way out.

"Of course it does," the stranger said. "I've come too far for anything else." He drew himself up a little straighter and said, "I am Loki, of Asgard, and I am burdened with glorious purpose."

"Loki?" Dr. Selvig said. He stood up from helping one of his fellow doctors, who was barely conscious. "Brother of Thor?"

"We have no quarrel with your people," Fury said.

Loki acknowledged Selvig and then returned his attention to Fury. "An ant has no quarrel with a boot," he said.

"Are you planning to step on us?" Fury asked. He already knew this encounter wasn't going to end well, but if he made it out, he needed to know as much about this Loki as possible.

"I come with glad tidings," Loki said. "Of a world made free."

"Free from what?" Fury asked.

Turning back to him, Loki said simply, "Freedom.

Freedom is life's great lie. Once you accept that in your heart…" As he spoke the word "heart," he turned and touched Selvig's chest with the tip of his scepter, just as he had with Hawkeye. Selvig gasped, and the same change came over his face that Fury had seen in Hawkeye's. "You will know peace."

No way was Nick Fury going to let this Loki get close enough to do that to him. "Yeah, you say peace," he said, "but I kind of think you mean the other thing."

Hawkeye had been looking around the complex. Now he stepped up to Loki. "Sir, Director Fury is stalling. This place is about to blow and drop a hundred feet of rock on us. He means to bury us."

Loki looked back at Fury, who said, "Like the pharaohs of old."

"He's right, the portal is collapsing in on itself!" Selvig called out from the monitors. "We've got maybe two minutes before this goes critical."

"Well then," Loki said. He glanced over at Hawkeye.

Without a word, Hawkeye drew his gun and shot Nick Fury once, dead center in the chest.

Fury went down without a sound. Loki, Selvig, Hawkeye, and another S.H.I.E.L.D. agent under Loki's control walked quickly out of the lab, Hawkeye carrying the steel briefcase. Inside it, the Tesseract glowed.

CHAPTER 2

Maria Hill saw Hawkeye come out of the lab into the garage with Selvig, a liaison officer, and a stranger carrying a spear. He looked more like one of the people they'd been recruiting into the Avengers Initiative than an ordinary technician or S.H.I.E.L.D. agent. "Who's that?" she asked.

"They didn't tell me," Hawkeye said.

The stranger got into the back of a light armored vehicle. The situation looked suspicious to Hill, but

Hawkeye was one of their most trusted operatives. She wasn't sure what to think.

Then her walkie-talkie crackled. "Hill," came Nick Fury's voice. "Barton has turned!"

She barely had time to dive for cover before Hawkeye was shooting at her. Selvig and the other S.H.I.E.L.D. agent were already in the truck. Hawkeye jumped into another vehicle, and they screeched out of the garage and up the ramp toward the surface. Hill fired after them, but her bullets pinged off the truck's armored exterior.

"They've got the Tesseract!" Fury radioed her. "Shut them down!"

She jumped into a jeep and headed after them. Other S.H.I.E.L.D. vehicles followed, filled with agents. They roared along the underground access road that led up to the surface in the New Mexico desert. She was gaining on them and firing as she drove. Sooner or later, she'd be close enough to have a good shot at the stranger.

He had other ideas, though. When he saw the pursuing convoy get too close, he pointed his scepter at them. The tip of it flared bright blue, and a bolt of energy lashed out from it, striking the vehicle in front of Hill and shattering the right side of its passenger compartment. The vehicle slewed around and flipped, rolling and landing sideways across the road. They were blocked.

At least most of them were. Hill bounced her jeep over a divider into an access road that ran parallel to the road Hawkeye was using. She stood on the gas and hoped she'd be able to cut him off before they got to the surface. Her walkie-talkie was a flurry of voices as Coulson continued to coordinate the evacuation. The energy field they'd created to hold the Tesseract was going to overload very soon.

She heard Coulson's voice: "We're clear upstairs, sir. We need to go." Did that mean Fury had gotten out of the lab? She couldn't stop to find out.

Hill shot out of the side road in front of Hawkeye's car. She yanked her jeep into a reverse slide, spinning it one hundred and eighty degrees so it was suddenly going backward, right in front of Hawkeye. She could see the surprise on his face. She shot at him, shattering both of their windshields. He fired back. Their bumpers met, and both of them nearly lost control—but Hawkeye had more drive going forward, and he forced her out of the way. She spun out, then slammed the jeep back into gear and took off after him again.

The blue orb of the Tesseract containment field collapsed into itself. There was a pause. Then all that energy exploded outward. The entire S.H.I.E.L.D. base heaved and collapsed into itself. The shock wave from the explosion buckled the road. Hill saw Hawkeye's vehicle ahead of the main wave, but she was caught right in it. Debris rained down on the road. She was close to the edge of the base, but she didn't know how much of it was going to collapse from the huge underground crater the explosion had created. She raced forward, hoping she would have enough time.